Opaline Allandet

I0654917

Godefroy the Cruel

Editions Dedicaces

GODEFROY THE CRUEL

[Godefroy le Cruel, translated from French by Caroline Andreea Zgortea]

Copyright © 2015 by Editions Dedicaces LLC

Published by:
Editions Dedicaces LLC
12759 NE Whitaker Way, Suite D833
Portland, Oregon, 97230
www.dedicaces.us

Library of Congress Cataloging-in-Publication Data
Allandet, Opaline
Godefroy the Cruel / by Opaline Allandet.
p. cm.
ISBN-13: 978-1-77076-469-9 (alk. paper)
ISBN-10: 1-77076-469-0 (alk. paper)

2

Opaline Allandet

Godefroy the Cruel

Table of contents

First part 9

Second part 23

Third part 37

Fourth part 47

Fifth part 65

Sixth part 85

It's easier to move a river
than to change your character.

First part

Godefroy IV of Lanicey paced back and forth along the guard room of the castle, that might have become a reception room. There, now, stood his young wife.

'Listen Mahaut, it's already been eight days since I have been trying to make you understand that it is of the upmost importance that I make this Crusade in the Holy Land. It is our duty that all the leaders of strongholds like ours leave to free Palestine, and especially Jerusalem of the Turk's occupation and of their accomplices. We have to fight these heretics and I must comply.

The young woman could only sigh once more.

'But why?' she answered. 'You have already been defeated in the Second Crusade.'

'Because we have succeeded in founding a county of Christians among the countries of the Middle East. And presently, this county has been taken back by the enemies. And don't forget that this Crusade was ordered by Pope Gregory VIII and preached by Bernard of Clairvaux.'

Mahaut was used to the numerous departures of her husband. In 1189, the epoch was still troubled by invaders, ravaging the county, not to mention the neighboring lords that often fought to enlarge their domain.

Godefroy was master of the fortress and felt invested by an imposing power: he was responsible to protect not only his family, and his domestic workers, but also all the inhabitants who worked for him, on his lands which he ran with a strong hand. It comprised mainly of peasants, woodcutters and all kinds of craftsmen, as well as their wives, who often lived in misery, surrounded by numerous brats to feed.

'Alas, I do not ignore it', repeated Mahaut, resigned. And I can only approve your undertaking. But, I do not know why, this departure doesn't seem like the others. You're going so far away! And for how long? I fear I will not see you again...'

She brought her hands in front of her eyes, like repelling a vision, her nature being so emotional.

Godefroy ceased his pacing and came close to her.

'Noble lady', he said, 'you musn't complain. I will serve for a great cause. You will be proud, believe me. And need I remind you that it's about an order of the Pope, sustained by the king? Only our God's law must triumph on this land.'

She raised sad eyes to him.

'It is unnecessary to remind me of all this' – Mahaut sighed again – 'but can you understand that your absence saddens me? It is so cold between these icy, dark walls! Only your presence can make me warm.'

Tears came to her eyes, and her face took a painful expression.

'I am very honored', answered Godefroy. 'But do not worry. I will return shortly, in a few months maybe. While waiting, I am counting on you to look after our children, especially over our son Quentin, guarantor of our lineage. On the other hand, if there is a point of importance, it is that of your fidelity. I know your beauty attracts all eyes on you, and I am very proud of this.'

'Oh my lord!' she replied in a tone full of reproach. 'How can you doubt my sincerity and my attachment to you?'

'I do not really doubt it. Still, because I do not know how long our separation will be, I ask you to swear your fidelity.'

The tone he used made the young woman shudder, knowing her husband didn't trifle with these things.

Mahaut remained stunned, she who had never paid attention to another man but him.

'Come, my lord, you can be certain.'

'All right, all right! We will leave in three days', he followed in an imperious voice. I have given all my instruction regarding the running of the domain to our steward. I had the horses cared for in view of this expedition. Have no worry, our servants are faithful to you and you can count on them in case of need. Furthermore, you have the chance to remain close to your father's lands (and this is what sealed our union), the Earl of Morenne, who became too old to fight. He will be able to watch over you and our property.'

Saying this, his grey eyes flashed a metallic luster, and his chin trembled of pride under his rugged black beard. Tall, very muscled thanks to his numerous physical exercises that he practiced often, he was imposing.

He pressed Mahaut against him for a moment, then walked away without looking back.

The Lanicey fortress was part of the oldest castles in Bourgogne, built in the time of the Merovigians and Carolingians. At the beginning, it consisted of large enclosures located on a high point, easily protected and whose walls were gradually reinforced. The fortified gateway was the only one fortified, opened between two circular towers, inspired by those of Roman legion camps. Inside, two or three successive enclosures were gradually furnished: the first one was reserved for the population of the surrounding villages, where they built a church, while the lord retired in the last one, where a high stone tower stood, accessible only in its first floor. This was, at the same time, a family residence and garrison barracks. Winters, long and cold in this region, accentuated more its austere character. The fortress was often enclosed in mist, and sometimes, its roofs and steeples seemed to emerge from the clouds, which rendered it even more mysterious.

Three days later, at dawn, Mahaut still couldn't succed in sleeping, tormented by a foreboding.

She heard the men cross the two enclosures of the fortress. A hubbub of happy, bold voices rose in concert, with the neighing of frantic horses. The young woman didn't know why she felt such an impression of tearing in her, as if a whole area of her life was collapsing.

It was the end of the twelfth century. Godefroy, accompanied by intrepid knights like him, launched into the third Crusade. Only the first one had been victorious. And fierce Christians had martyred their enemies, tortured like animals. Some, had been skewered alive and, it was said, eaten.

The second Crusade had revealed itself to be disastrous for the king that led it: Louis VII, king of Franks, and the German emperor, Conrad III. The Crusaders had won Jerusalem, but they had failed at the gates of Damascus, not succeding in crossing the siege. After their return in the West, their failure had provoked violent movements within the church and the army in different countries of Europe. It was necessary, at all costs, to defeat these unbelievers.

So it was with enthusiasm and determination they rushed there, in 1189, under Philippe August's command, recently crowned king of the Franks, Frédéric Barbarossa, successor of Conrad III, and Richard Lion-Heart, king of England. Frédéric Barbarossa had provoked Saladin, master of the Byzantine Empire to a duel, but he drowned accidentally while crossing a river in 1190, before fighting him. The kings had gathered important military troops, led by knights like baron Lanicey.

For Mahaut, life had to continue. She felt divided between the hope of this Crusade being victorious and the sadness of the separation from her husband, for whom she felt attachment.

The young woman brought all her attention to the education of her children, Quentin and Lidwine, like the lord had commanded. Quentin, aged fourteen, seemed to possess his father's courage, without having his excessive character. And Lidwine, two years his junior, combined her mother's beauty with a strong personality. Quentin's education was intrusted to a tutor who knew how to read, write and count. So, he taught him, in addition to civic education, the elementary basis of writing and calculation. Lidwine, even though she was just a girl, benefited from this courses as well.

Baroness Lanicey found them each day, at the time of meals taken together, and let herself be distracted by their heedlessness and laughter. While the cold wasn't so intense, she walked in company of Lidwine in the village that lay at the feet of the fortress. When they appeared, the peasants bowed to greet them, without interrupting their hard work: they were under Ulric's surveillance, a supervisor with an iron fist, reputed to be without soul.

'Do you think we'll know one day the end of these stupid wars that only take lives and feed our fears?' Mahaut asked her daughter.

Lidwine didn't know what the answer to these questions was, who surpassed her. But she possessed a capital advantage, that of youth discovering life, and who breathed the surrounding smells of spring.

'Of course!' answered the little girl, rising her golden little face to her mother.

Often, the mistress of Lanicey climbed to the highest point of the tower, watching with hope the whereabouts of riders who passed by the fortress. From there, one could overlook the valleys and forests and allowed to see the enemy as soon as he came. The guards ended up accepting the presence of the baroness at their sides. The gusts of icy wind engulfed the loopholes and became like bites on the face of the young woman. She was certain of the return of her husband...

Like every year, at the end of the harvesting, when barns and granaries overflowed with wheat, rye, barley, apples and various fruits, the Earl of Morenne, Mahaut's father, organized a great feast in his castle. All the neighboring squires were invited, as well as their spouses, parents and friends who possessed a title of nobility. Many ladies took this chance to parade in their finery. As for the lords, young or old, they posted their emblazones on their arms, swords or carved daggers, gleaming swords, as if there was a tournament.

Mahaut had refused to attend last year. Then, the count succeeded in convincing her this year.

She went without her husband for the first time. Clothed in a black dress that highlighted her clear complexion, she wore an encrusted belt with white pearls which encircled her slim waist. The same pearls gleamed at her ears, at her neck and on her wrists. Her long hair, of a pale blond, wrapped around her neck, was held by a cap of black tulle, giving her a sort of tragic aura. Mahaut mainly stood away from the couples she knew, who chatted happily among them.

The meal was hearty and well watered because the harvest had proved abundant in the year 1191. And as the wine exalted them, the diners' laughter rang out from everywhere. The evening was animated by dances and songs, by the sounds of the hurdy-gurdy and harps, in the light of torches. The atmosphere became magical: the dancers' cheeks reddened with vermilion, and the eyes of the gentlemen sparkled with desire, sudden or awakened. Some of them slipped away discreetly in annex chambers provided for gallant games between men or women, according to their inclinations.

An unknown knight had remarked Mahaut and he invited her to dance, and she dared not refuse.

He could admire the lady's suppleness, as well as her elegance. At first suspicious, reserved, then dazed by this air of gaiety, she relaxed little by little, a smile lighted her beautiful face, and her blue eyes became shining.

'May I ask you a question, Madam?'

'It depends which one…'

But he continued.

'How come a beautiful lady like yourself is unaccompanied? Are you a widow?' Inquired viscount Parroux, devouring her with a knowing eye.

'I find you to be very curious in my regard!' She answered for appearance's sake, but in reality, not unhappy.

'Oh! It's just that my heart is conquered by your beauty and I am most troubled', added the viscount.

Mahaut, even though she wasn't insensitive to this flattery, didn't answer. She thought about Godefroy, who wouldn't have liked her to abandon herself in the arms of another man but him… for he was extremely jealous. And an uncontrollable tremor escaped her.

Feeling her moved, the viscount took courage.

'Are you cold, dear lady? Do you want a glass of hot wine?'

And the knight already pulled her to a servant who poured drinks.

'I do want one, sire. But it is nothing, just a light discomfort, and I just want to sit.'

'Then allow me, Madam, to sit by your side.'

She sat down on a sofa and the viscount took care to spread her dress.

'Without wanting to seem indiscreet', he insisted however, 'may I know what has you in this state?'

Mahaut hesitated a little, but she felt the need to confide, maybe after drinking a little too much wine.

'I was thinking of my dear husband who is engaged in the current Crusade, and of which we do not know if it will end.'

'Come, Madam!' Exclaimed the viscount. 'Far be it from me to frighten you! But do you not know that three-quarters of these valiant warriors have been decimated by the Turks and they will not come back?'

'My God! Is this possible!' Moaned the baroness, becoming pale all of a sudden.

'Unfortunately!' Continued the knight. 'I am very saddened to give you such news! I myself just came back as my leg was injured and I couldn't ride anymore. I know others who have died, after having endured worse pains!'

And the viscount Parroux cited the names of gentlemen who were known to have been slain in the Holy Land.

Mahaut barely heard these names, such anxiety did she feel!

'But then', she rebelled after a moment, ' why didn't my father, who is the host of this castle, inform me of this?'

He encircled the shoulders of the young woman with a protective, gentle hold.

'Maybe he did not wish to hurt you, something I can easily understand? You seem so fragile!'

Mahaut remained lost in her thoughts. Then, finding the use of her feet again, she decided to go back home.

She sincerely thanked viscount Parroux, who had enchanted and then tarnished her evening.

'Will you allow me, dear lady, to visit you, it will only be to know if you are feeling better?' he dared ask.

Of a firm voice, but with a sweet intonation, she answered.

'I am sorry, sire, but I can not. Will you please excuse me.'

With a weak smile, she took leave of him.

Before disappearing, she approached Earl Morenne, her father. This one, a widow for two years, was heavily surrounded by noble ladies who were not yet taken, at more than twenty-five years of age.

'Father', she murmured, 'I allow myself to take of leave you, thanking you for inviting me. I would dearly wish to talk to you, as soon as it will be possible for you to come to my dwelling.'

'Is it urgent?' Inquired the earl. 'What is happening!'

Before Mahaut's embarassed air, he understood that he musn't insist.

'Of course, dear child', he said, depositing a light kiss on her forehead. 'I will come tomorrow, at the beginning of the afternoon. See you soon!'

The young baroness felt a little relieved at the idea of being able to confide in her father.

Around two in the afternoon, the next day, Earl Morenne, who was an excellent rider, rushed to his daughter's and found her prostrated on her settee.

'What is it, my dear Mahaut, for me to find you thus afflicted? Were you not delighted with my party, which, they told me, was a great success with the knights of our county?'

'Of course, Father, it was very successful, I agree. Still, talking about knights, precisely, I need your enlightenment.'

While he took place in a high wooden chair covered with red velvet, the young woman gathered her courage and followed.

'Yes, Father, it is about my husband.'

It was not the first time she addressed this subject with him. But she had more information. And she told him about her conversation with viscount Parroux.

'You know to which point I am attached to my lord: I have a lot of esteem for him and I admire his courage. But it will be almost two years since his departure and not having any news of him, I am afraid that…'

'That he is not of this world anymore?' Continued the earl. 'It is a question I have constantly been asking myself for several months. But I fear you have no other choice but await his return. Not having been recognized among the dead, nothing allows us to think he is gone. You must always hope.'

'Of ourse, Father, but in this case, where can he be?'

'Maybe he is held prisoner? Only God knows…'

Mahaut lowered her head, having to resign herself to fate. Then she continued.

'I must confess, as well, something that is in my heart: Godefroy is an excellent husband and I think he loves me in his own way, that is to say, without showing it. And this lack of affection, of warmth, of which I am in such need, has failed me. I do not know how to explain what I am feeling, but it inspires a strange feeling that scares me.'

'Come, Mahaut, you are too sentimental! I think your husband is the one you need, for he knows what he wants. He has the strong character of those men who have will. I can understand that solitude weighs upon you, for I realize this after the death of your dear mother. God have her soul, for she deserves it! But life is made of unexpected to be overcome and you must conform yourself.'

The young woman turned to the window and seemed absorbed by the contemplation of nature that began to color in tones of rust and orange: autumn approached, inevitably. She could see the small chapel, behind an alley planted with firs.

She went there daily to demand God's benevolance and ask for the return of her knight.

'Listen', continued to earl, trying to console her, 'I want to try something for you. This is my idea: I will go to the Duke of Bourgogne, who is my overlord and whose power is recognised all over. I will ask him to make inquiries concerning your husband. I will give him money if need be.'

'Oh, father!' Cried Mahaut, her face suddenly illuminated, 'I thank you from the bottom of my heart.'

And she threw herself in his arms to express her joy.

The duke of Bourgogne accepted this request and sent his men to make inquiries to the Holy Land, through the prelates. But these remained futile.

Shortly after receiving the Earl of Morenne, Waldemar, the older and most faithful servant of the Lanicey fortress, stood before the Baroness saying:

'Very noble Lady, a lord presented himself to the first gate of the enclosure. The guards wanted to stop him, but this knight got upset, saying he knows you. Should I let him in?'

Mahaut felt torn between the desire to see again the viscount who had charmed her unwittingly that evening, and the fear of introducing an enemy of her lord in the castle. She contemplated the garden in the hope of seeing the one who dared impose himself so. Then, tired of loneliness, she decided to let him in. Her heart beating, the young woman ordered Waldemar to see him in. It was not easy, as he had to cross the two enclosures of the fortress.

In a hurry, she climbed in her apartment to change into her most beautiful attire: a blue dress, matching the color of her eyes. She put a sapphire necklace to her neck, inherited from her late mother, which gave her more shine. Her long blond hair was intertwined with blue velvet ribbons. She seemed like an angel from a painting.

While she descended the stairs that led to the reception hall, Waldemar came to talk to her apart.

'Very noble Lady, I think this knight is not known to us.'

'But maybe he is known by me?' She heard herself answer without thinking.

While she opened the door leading to a small salon where the servants had set him, Mahaut laid eyes on viscount Parroux, who had an admirative and bold look.

After the servants left, the young baroness found more reasonable to scold him gently.

'Lord Parroux…'

'Excuse me for interrupting, Madam, but do call me rather Aymeric…'

'Didn't I strictly forbid you to see me again, after taking leave of you at my father's?' She tried to take on an outraged face, to mask the beatings of her heart who betrayed a certain feeling of pleasure on her part. But the viscount was not to be impressed.

'Dear Lady, if I permitted myself to breach your interdiction, it was to let you know that one of my cousins returned from Palestine, being wounded in his turn...'

Mahaut couldn't help herself from jumping on the settee, so great was her desire to see the Lord of Lanicey again!

'May I ask if he met my husband there? Is he still alive?'

She held her breath for a moment, in all that waiting.

'My cousin, whom I have questioned in this regard, unfortunately couldn't answer. He knows that your Lord has fought with great courage against the infidels. He confided that during a battle, particularly deadly, he dissappeared... But it was impossible for him to say if he was dead or still alive, for his body was never found...

The face of the baroness became very anxious and tears blurred her eyes.

'When did your cousin see him for the last time?'

'It was at the siege of Damascus which lasted for months. Maybe he was buried under the ruins?'

After a sigh that said about her disappointment, Mahaut, a good hostess, ordered a servant to bring them their best wine to give a drink to the Lord of Parroux. This one contemplated the young woman, seated before him and he felt drunk, not by alcohol, but by her presence only.

In that moment, in came Lidwine, to show her mother the results of her marks obtained in dictation and, naturally, made her best reverence before the viscount, in greeting.

Aymeric felt very flattered and was full of praise for the small lady. This one, from the top of her fourteen springs, was not insensible to the charms of men. After being ecstatic for her notes, the baroness sent her daughter out of the small salon.

Aymeric of Parroux, curiously, had remained unmarried, and still, this was not from lack of ladies, whom

20

he adored seduce. But the baroness wasn't looking to know this, respecting his silence on the subject.

The moment came when the viscount had to retire, and it was not without difficulty, for everything in the castle enchanted him. His was more recently built and didn't have enclosures.

Nevertheless, it was erected on a hill too.

He rose at sunset and thanked Mahaut warmly for her pleasant reception. She held out her hand to kiss, when he burned to take her into his arms, but he remained courteous.

'It was a real pleasure for me', he declared. 'My castle is not so far from yours. Thereby, can I beg a favour of you?'

Mahaut, with a sensible heart, blushed.

'Still, tell me.'

'I would wish so much, since I feel you alone (he was referring to the absence of Godfrey) to come back from time to time to greet you!'

The young woman stayed silent for a long moment, torn between her heart and her reason, but after two heavy years of solitude, she let herself be induced by her heart....

'If it is only this, lord, I can allow it.'

Aymeric of Parroux returned home with the hope of conquering her.

For two or three months, Aymeric returned to the fortress of Lanicey, attracted by the grace and sweetness of Mahaut. At first, he forced himself to keep their relation on a purely amical level. But the viscount had to admit that a stronger feeling pushed him towards her, and against which he could not fight. On her side, the baroness felt tortured between the duty and fidelity to her husband, probably dead, and this strange friendship that bothered her... The viscount became, little by little, indispensable. How to resist against all those delicate attentions made by the gentleman? In fact, he never came with empty hands, sometimes offering her wild flowers, sometimes delicacies made by his cooks.

21

When she sat down, he took pains to put cushions around her, like a precious stone in its case. When leaving, Mahaut dared not refuse them, for fear of offending him. Then, she received them with evident pleasure.

At this stage, the baroness dared ask him the reason for not being married yet.

'Well', he answered, 'when I was an adolescent, I fell in love with a young lady of a superior social rank than mine, who had been promised to a great German lord. Even if she showed herself not to be insensible to my feelings, the young girl disappeared one day in a castle in Bavaria, among the dark forests across the Rhine and her memory has haunted me for a long time! I then refused all the contenders my father never ceased to present me. But I prefered to make myself known in wars, looking in the honors a certain compensation to what I once felt like contempt.'

One morning, while they sat together at the heights of the fortress, still bathed in persistent mists, they felt the strange sensation of being in a magical place, unknown to them and they felt lost in the skies... Mahaut reached out to support herself against the wooden ramp. Aymeric held out his hand to help her and approached her body eagerly.

'Sweet and beautiful friend', he told her, 'will you allow me to make a confession that has burned in me for a long time? I love you, with a strong and loyal love, and...'

Mahaut didn't try to free herself from the embrace and whispered:

'And I truly think that I share the same feeling as you...'

Little by little, viscount Parroux was admitted by all the inhabitants of the Lanicey castle, for it seemed to come alive. They began to respect and admire him like he was a true lord. And no one seemed shocked when he became the lover of the too tender Mahaut.

Second part

A year later, one day, a cloud of dust was noticed in the distance by the faction lookouts from the guard tower of the Lanicey fortress. They heard a noise of gallop increasing, almost making the earth tremble.

Who could well take down the valley, at that speed, and unannounced? Was it a new barbarian invasion, as they had become frequent, under a land not yet unified by the same banner?

How great was the surprise of the rider being the lord of the lands, for it was him who was coming back, after three years of absence, when he stopped to the drawbridge of the castle!

The guards, who recognised his spirit and his high stature, hesitated a moment before raising them. Some were unknown to Godefroy, but this could be explained: his absence had been so long! He felt very happy to find them again, these brave men!

'Whoa!' he cried powerfully while slowing his horse who reared. 'What are you waiting for to let in your Lord and Master?' And he slammed his whip in the air.

Old Waldemar, who had known him since his childhood, showed an anxious and embarrassed face.

'Confound it!' screamed Godefroy, 'what is the meaning of this?'

His haste to find Lady Mahaut of blond hair was great: he had missed her so! The refined nonchalance and sensuality of oriental women, whom he had frequented at certain brothels, that were flourishing there, had greatly excited him. But none of them had the grace and the small fragility his wife had. He could finally take her in his arms, and his children who by now had to be big and would be his pride!

Certain soldiers welcomed him with the eagerness he expected, apparently happy with his return. But, advancing in the courtyard, he remarked men who, instead of saluting him, retired themselves inside the dwellings. When he jumped from his horse and wanted to and tried to cross the wooden gate of the castle, he found it closed.

A tremor of rage ran along his spine and he let out a whole string of expletives. he banged furiously against the gate with his fists of steel, then, seeing that no one opened the door, with a saber blow, he shattered the bolt of the door: it gave in under his increased strength. He overthrew Waldemar, the old servant who had stayed posted behind the door. And without making excuses, he asked:

'Come, Waldemar, what is happening here?'

The old man couldn't answer, with his breath cut.

Godefroy climbed running the wooden staircase, which was used to get to Mahaut's apartment. He crossed terrified servants on his way, but he did not see them. The baroness was receiving her love that day, for he had come back from a voyage and the servants had received the order to open to no one. Aymeric, after savouring the delicacies of a passionate loving, was relaxing in a pleasant moment of torpor.

Still, a servant had succeeded in warning them, on the sly, of the return of the lord. When Aymeric heard this, he had just enough time to dress, and to try to disappear through the window. But it was a lost cause: already Godefroy was forcing he door to his unfaithful wife's room, and found her trembling in her bed.

Such was her amazement, that she fell, floored.

Then, coming back to his senses, the blood of the lord began to boil. He recognised a friend, neighbouring his territory, Aymeric of Parroux, the traitor who had flouted while he had continued to wage the war in the crusade. His chest swelled under his armour, not yer removed, that it

24

seemed too narrow! His nostrils, resembling those of a mad horse, throbbed inordinately. It was then that a hoarse cry, like that of a hungry wolf escaped from his throat.

'Parroux', he screamed, 'you are dead, like a sewer rat! I'll pull your guts to the air, traitor!'

And putting his words into action, he lowered his sword so strongly that he beheaded him in one sweep: Aymeric hadn't had the time to jump through the window. How many enemies had had the same fate, in the Middle East? He didn't know.

The lord's rage not being yet quenched, he exclaimed:

'Ah! How I regret to not have slain you on the field! I would have enjoyed so hearing you cry under torture!'

Mahaut couldn't help herself scream in her turn, seeing her lover decapitated.

Godefroy turned to his wife and threw Aymeric's head on her knees, sneering.

'Look, bitch! You can kiss him as much as you like, for in a few moments I will cut him in pieces under your eyes!'

Mahaut was terrorized and she closed her eyes, unable to see this carnage. Two fellows were ordered to hold her firmly by the shoulders so she could not shrink from this sight… Soon, the walls of the room were covered in blood that dripped on the stairs…

The servants and the household staff, terrorized so by his barbarity, had taken refuge in the stable and implored the sky so that their dear mistress would be spared.

Then, the lord of Lanicey let his hatred against Mahaut, for she had terribly hurt him in his love and his ego. He approached her and screamed.

'Just you wait, bitch, your turn will come!'

It was the first time he addressed her on familiar terms, and the sweet Mahaut felt it as her death sentence.

Godefroy turned to the guards who had recognised him.

'Guards! Take hold of this bitch so she won't escape. And it will be her who will be tortured, for she has betrayed me under my own roof! On all the devils, I swear that only my vengeance will be able to calm me.'

His proud lips were rolled by a sneer of contempt and he threw to her face.

'Mahaut, you're nothing but a bitch and you deserve to die as well. Ah! How I have been wrong to marry you, for I thought you virtuous!'

He slapped her on both cheeks. The young woman fell at his feet, shedding bitter tears.

'Lord, have pity of me! Grace! You have to listen to me!'

But he would listen only to his rage, resembling a torrent swollen by a storm, and who had become devastating.

'Lord! I ask forgiveness with all my heart', implored Mahaut, 'but everyone here thought you were killed. We made inquiries and I waited for you for so long, in vain…'

But the lord didn't let himself be softened.

'Shut up, you're only a whore!'

In his rage, he snatched all her clothes and didn't notice her splendid nude body. He grabbed her by her long undone hair and pulled her out of the room (that had been theirs) in the corridor, then along the wooden rough stairs. Her skin, very fine and sensitive, flayed by this brutality, left bloody traces along the way.

'Lord! Forgive me!' Sobbed the young woman, between two howls of pain...

'No! I will never forgive you!' Vociferated Godefroy. 'I am leading you to a dungeon where you will rot slowly, day after day. This will already be your coffin.'

After a long agonizing cry, that must have resonated until the bottom of the valley, she finally lost consciousness. Her lord could thus command two guards to transport her in the darkest, most isolated dungeon of the fortress, usually reserved for criminals.

The next morning, after having called for help in vain, and moaned all night, endless for her, broken by terror and tiredness, Mahaut understood that her husband would not give in: she was sentenced to end here, abandoned by all.

They had thrown her a black frock for clothing and a pair of stockings of coarse wool.

She couldn't help herself to think of her two children, whom she would not see again, and who found themselves under the rule of that monster. On the other hand, the young woman felt haunted by the horrible vision of Aymeric's bloody head on her knees. She had the feeling of still feeling him… Thanks to him, she had tasted wonderful moments, and even if this would cost her her life, Mahaut didn't regret anything. But the young woman felt incredibly responsible for the death of lord Parroux, for he had only loved her…

She didn't feel the hunger, only the intense thirst that leads to intense anxiety.

Exhausted, she sank down on the straw that served as her bed and ended up falling into a deep sleep.

After the sweet Mahaut had been buried in her dungeon and her lover decapitated, cut to pieces, Godefroy felt relieved of a great weight: he was again the undisputed master of the house. His household staff called him among them "Godefroy the Cruel".

His fury abandoned him gradually, like a wave lifted by a cyclone, crashing against the rocks, then sprawling on the shore. But he was not appeased for all that! Every day, he pondered on his shame that the disorderly conduct of his wife had imposed to him, the most courageous of warriors and to his people! For all the inhabitants, even the most poor, had to mock him, not openly, of course, otherwise he would have hanged more than a braggart! But among the attendants and the people in the stable, not to mention the servants, who were nothing but gossips, their tongues would go well underway. And so, he was obliged to dismiss those who had shown themselves unfaithful upon his return.

Even his confessor who frequently visited, trying to convert him to clemency, and who exhorted him in his prayers, trying to get him to show some clemence, had to admit that the mood of the lord had not changed.

'Finally, sire!' Vainly begged the priest, 'your wife has sinned, this is certain. But I know the bottom of her heart: I know her heart and her conscience, that she did not betray you. She thought, like everyone here, that you were dead.

'Ah! You too?' - and the baron sprang from his armchair – 'are you part of the traitors?'

The priest was afraid, scared of being fired and sent to a nameless abbey.

'Of course not! Calm down, my lord! Then again, this event could have taken place. Only God is master of our destiny, and we can't know it, poor wretches that we are.'

'I do not believe in your nonsense!' Sneered the sire. 'I remain mortally humiliated, finding myself, furthermore, a great one of this kingdom: this is why, I have to set an example: in showing myself RUTH-LESS.

Are you going to make the apology of the devil and of his false works? While throwing these words: "Honor before anything", this is my standard!'

And he pounded the ground with his long metal boots that crunched at every step.

'Just like my ancestors, of whom you can admire the portraits here: they were the ones who told me what road to follow…'

The priest cast a quick eye on these portraits that he knew well, but who froze him: for their expressions said nothing good to him.

It was in that time that the baron of Lanicey felt the need to reinforce his authority and to acquire some supplementary riches. He took the example of his ancestors that hadn't hesitated in tracking the traders. They borrowed the path that surrounded his stronghold to sell their goods.

Some hawked fabrics, precious objects, as well as pieces of gold, en route to Lombardy: it had clever bankers whose tricks were well known, and this country served a bit like a rotating board rotating to enrich the powerful of this world.

When carriers were announced, in order to adjust their toll (this existed already in the Roman era) they were always courteously invited by Ulric, the supervisor of the Lanicey castle. He proposed them a drink in his company, to make a little stop. He praised the unspeakable delight of their vineyards, abundant in the area.

Near a good wooden fire that danced in the fireplace of the old kitchen, Ulric clinked glasses with unbelieving merchants. They, ignorant that they were the victims of a trap, shared, delighted, the pot of friendship. Then, after a while, as they felt sick and shaky, Ulric called a henchman: between the two of them, they transported them in a neighboring room where a bed concealing a trap was found. When the poison had done its work, it was enough to open the trap. It overlooked a secret underground fortress opening on a spring. Once fallen, the bodies were driven by this spring, also underground, before flowing into the river that wound below the rocks. The baron could become richer this way, reselling the precious objects, which allowed him to repair his tower.

Still, at the end of some months, his humiliation was less and less present, Godefroy emerged from this strange torpor that had knocked him all of a sudden, so great had been the shock to him! His rancor faded a bit, and the following spring, life resumed his rights over him. At first, sap got into his body and his mind.

He first decided to get drunk on fresh air: he made long rides on horseback, being an excellent rider, alone across the forests, the fields bordered by lakes and dotted with wild flowers, for miles that he did not measure, stunned by exhilarating sensations. He went down to a cave where the water was so blue that no one could understand this natural phenomenon: it was an enchanting place that calmed him at then end of the race.

The lord was sometimes accompanied by his son, Quentin. But he followed him against his will, not being able to take the retaliation he had done to his mother.

'My son, you will soon be a man, and you have no longer need of your mother', he said to him tapping him on the shoulder.

Then he took to frequent the taverns, where the keepers didn't hesitate in filling his cup with a red and rough wine. There was a joyous, bawdy atmosphere, that reinvigorated him. He even found certain companions of weapons from his youth, against whom he had crossed swords. These, having become idle between the two wars, gave themselves to practicing games and women.

It was then that Godefroy turned to the girls with prominent hips and overflowing corsages who served drinks and who indulged in some debauchery with drunken rascals, no matter their rang in society. A desire for the flesh devoured him.

He raised his eyes to the women surrounding him at the castle. There were all sorts of servants: the cooks, the women employed to clean, the maids, and even a young woman of the gentry, Aliénor, whose father had died at his side during a terrible battle against the barbarians. This man had been a widower for several years, Aliénor, aged twelve at that time, would have been an orphan. This poor child had seen her mother die before her eyes, raped by bandits and she remained traumatized. Then, he confided his girl to Godefroy who, by pity, accepted to become her guardian. Her father had placed her in a convent of the Bénédictines. At the end of two years, the lord brought her to his fortress, where she kept Lidwine company.

Among the servants, he noticed one whose mother had once been in his service. The latter being deceased, Jacotte had taken over her mother's humble functions naturally, and did them very well indeed.

Godefroy arranged with Ulric, his heartless servant, to remain alone with her. Ulric, on his side, feared nothing while debauchery was concerned for a long time.

One morning, while Jacotte was serving him a very hearty meal, the baron could admire everything of the show of her breasts leaning over him. He noticed that they were free and attractive, under the light black material that brought out the whiteness of their skin. Benefiting from the insolence of her youth, proud of the arch of her loins, the servant didn't lower her long silky lashes before the bold eyes of the lord. Thereby, Godefroy examined more closely this Jacotte, insisting on her promising formes, but she was not frightened by the unduly examination.

He then felt exhilarated before this pretty face, this bounced body, which made him think of a young chick, that he would have wanted to taste! For the fat wenches that could be found in the back rooms of taverns that could sufficiently sate him… And then, this Jacotte was at the grip of his hands, according to his good natural urges for a healthy man to have, and which seized him suddenly.

Still with Ulric's complicity, the lord arranged to make her work in his apartment, so he could leer at leisure her generous baits, without having to move. The beautiful servant, which was not at all foolish, swayed in such a way when she came to draw the draperies of the windows for the first time, that him, not being able to hold out any longer, caught her by an arm and pulled her to him.

'But tell me, Jacotte, you have become a beautiful plant now!'

Not only was the young girl not intimidated, but she squirmed so that her blouse fell, releasing her beautiful and firm breasts. Then Godefroy laid her on his bed and when he wanted to truss her, he discovered that the privacy of the beauty was not even veiled by the smallest fabric. He threw himself over her, then in her, and enjoying himself he cried very loudly:

'By God! It's good!'

It was only after he asked the question.

'You most surely must have more than one boy in your petticoats, among the young people who are employed here ... hummmmmmmmm?'

'Oh, no my Lord! They are too ugly for me!' She answered putting on her dress.

'Listen to me well', he added all of a sudden, 'I want you to come every evening to prepare by bed.'

Then, Jacotte's cheeks reddened by a pleasure that she did not hide.

Then, every evening, without any precaution of confidentiality, for everyone knew that the master could enjoy his servants, Godefroy wallowed in an indescribable pleasure, such was Jacotte's felinity that awakened new needs in him.

He felt younger with at least fifteen years and that had the happy consequence of softening a bit his warlike state. In short, he thought less and less of crushing his neighbours.

No one thought of complaining except for his daughter Lidwine, that at the beginning of her sixteen years, showed herself revolted by the casual attitude of her father. If she had to tolerate the masculine supremacy, that could degrade himself without fear of being misjudged, she boiled with indignation at the idea that her father, depraved in this way, had locked up her mother for a mistake of which she was innocent.

She too, like the Lord of Lanicey, had a grudge and didn't hesitate to express her rage.

'Father, how can you show yourself so disloyal to your wife that lies in the worst dungeon?'

'It is not your place to criticize my acts, Lidwine. Every girl must respect her father, beginning with you. Didn't I already teach you this? These stories do not concern you.'

'Yes, they do!' she cut in, 'for they are about my mother!'

The lord then turned the conversation.

'You would best get ready to take a husband, and it is what I shall employ myself to find for you presently'.

She frowned impatiently.

'By all means, do not go to all this trouble! I will be perfectly able to find him myself...'

'Are you then ignorant of the fact that a daughter must marry a man chosen by her father? And I know, among my friends, some great catches that will make a princess out of you.'

'I have no need of them: there are plenty of young and beautiful men among our neighbours. And I will ask God that he will be nothing like you.'

'All the same, he will have to be. But I dearly love seeing you in this state, when you are resplendent with rage, as you are for sure my dignified daughter!'

Jacotte, on her side, was the object of countless jealousies and gossips from the part of the other servants. But they didn't show them openly, fearing that they will be heard by the lord and lose their employ.

Misery reigned in the villages: many people died of hunger, of cold, or of exhaustion in the hard works that barely left them with what to feed their offsprings. The women died young, giving birth too often, and not keeping but three or four children: three-quarters of which died before the age of two. The servants of the lord of Lanicey didn't dare complain, for they were housed and properly nourished, and could find a husband without any trouble.

Unfortunately for the beautiful Jacotte, she discovered after some time that she was pregnant. This was a catastrophe for her, for she knew that Godefroy would never accept to recognise this child. When se revealed her state to the lord and alluded to its paternity, after a voluptuous embrace, the latter rose anew.

'Nothing can prove it to me and I am even certain that you were with more than one man when you're heat... !'

'Oh! How can you believe this, me how loves you more than anyone. I can swear it!'

'It's this!' he said, 'I know well what oaths mean!' (and he thought of Mahaut).

Godefroy felt annoyed by this domestic problem which he did not need.

The lion began to roar in him. He paced his room furiously, throwing randomly objects that he encountered in his path. The servants, intrigued by this racket, posted themselves behind the door to listen and laugh quietly.

'I will never recognise this bastard', he screamed, 'even if I am the father! For with women, are we ever sure of anything? They are only artful whores. Then, do you know what remains to be done, my beauty?'

And his look, like a vulture, already pierced her.

'You'll clear out of here,' he shouted, 'and the sooner the better.'

Upon hearing these terrible words, Jacotte couldn't help a tremor at the idea of being locked up like her old mistress, in a sombre dungeon of this castle, two years had already passed ...

'Don't worry, my lord. But give me a few days, the time to pack.'

Three days after this memorable scene, Godefroy saw moving away, in the early morning, deep in the misty valley, a chariot driven by an old stallion. The animal seemed to struggle to pull that load.

Finally relieved by Jacotte's leaving, the baron returned to the gambling den to truss new wenches.

At the end of these two years, the beautiful Mahaut didn't have the appearance of a lady anymore, not even that of a woman… Her harmonious body had become unrecognizable, emaciated and dirty, rotting in a foul dungeon, humid and barely lighted.

The ignoble image of her beloved beheaded, then cut into pieces before her, haunted her day and night, for if she dazed a little, the image came into her nightmares. But she didn't regret anything, except the presence of her children.

Mahaut had moved back to her window as to withdraw from life. Every day, she went down a little further into hell, weighed down by grief. The young woman had to stay bent constantly, the vault, built into the rock, was so low. Her bust had broken into two. She had back pains all the time and didn't dare move anymore.

The rats had gnawed the lower part of her aba, which had become a rag and in winter she shivered with cold, not feeling her members. In cold temperatures, very common in the Jurassian region, they threw her a blanket in which she barely managed to roll.

Mahaut had ceased to call for someone to come to her aide, had ceased to moan, or even to try to implore her guards. Godefroy had recruited them among the cruelest of his soldiers, devoid of any human feeling. One of them, who had dared take pity of the fate of the poor woman, had been dismissed on the spot. All others, impassive, performed their tasks without any qualms: they brought her daily some crusts of stale bread, all accompanied by a a water pitcher. Or they changed her litter from time to time. She had become the same as an animal!

The harsh winter hung gigantic ice cubes near the grating. When they managed to melt, late in the gray and rainy spring sky, the water flowed along the walls of her prison and formed mold.

Third part

Lidwine's assertive beauty, going on her sixteenth spring, began to torment her father. He had but one idea in his head: to marry her. After all, he thought, she was at an age to marry and the effect would be to distance her numerous sighing young suitors that made sweet eyes at her in the neighbourhood.

It would be an easy affair to conclude, taking into account that she would be provided with a good dowry, not unimportant to a gentleman, obviously.

For his son, heir to the stronghold, he had other views: he will find him a young girl of hight nobility to rebuild his blazon.

To come back to Lidwine, Godefroy had thought that, rather than letting her fall in love with a young dove with no future, it would be more sensible for him to exploit his daughter's beauty, in order to expand his territory. Wasn't it a gift from the skies to have such a beautiful girl? Didn't religion teach, to whomever wanted to listen, that it was a duty to grow the gifts the Supreme Master had given you?

With this decision, the only thing left was to form an alliance with a lord whose lands were far enough away from his, and that was it.

In that time, at the reign of Philip Augustus, son of Louis XII, the county of Bourgogne, which included the Lanicey fortress, was not yet attached to the Capetian dynasty. The king of France, although he strived to conquer it, as well as other counties, had failed in this matter. The Burgundians had suffered all kinds of invasions. The

Burgundians, among others, came from Scandinavia, and left their name. This county was attached to the Holy German Empire, as were all the counties situated in the East of France.

Philip Augustus, king of France, was firstly allied to Richard the Lion-Heart, king og England, to help the last to overthrow his father's throne. They participated together in the third Crusade, accompanied by Frédéric Barbarossa, German emperor, that had drowned there. Philip Augustus came back to France in 1191 and made war with Richard the Lion-Heart to seize his Aquitaine lands, searching to enrich the French territory.

Godefroy darted devoutly in this crusade, as he loved waging wars and serving his Emperor. The Burgundian nobles, like the Burgundian people, revealed themselves to be particularly warlike, reckless, bold, and showed their legendary courage. Their countless scars, wounds and bruises that covered them, were exhibited with great pride. Besides, this gave them a certain prestige in the eyes of the noble ladies, who swooned with admiration for them. During this Crusade where the Lord of Lanicey fought the Turks, before liberating Jerusalem of the infidels, he lost many of his valuable companions, affected by the same ardor as his.

But he also made new solid friendships with other warriors who had come from different points of the West: Latins, British, French or German lords who belonged to another county than his.

It was only in 1366 that another part of the county of Burgundy took the name of Franche-Comté. It was on the lands of the Levant, where during a very bloody fight, the baron of Lanicey became friends with the Duke of Sacht. The duke had inherited from his German uncle a stronghold in the Nivernais County and had thereby a fortified house in Var.

Godfrey was going to be rammed by a Turk, when Otto of Sacht, with a swing of his sword, threw the enemy's saber. It was a miracle. For the baron would have had his throat cut. Becoming grateful to his unexpected saviour, Godefroy followed him and joined him in his camp, this explaining his disappearance to his old Jura companions in arms.

By pure chance, Godefroy was invited to a party organized by the Count of Cravadem, one of his neighbours, in his wonderful castle. It was constructed in a very picturesque scene: perched on a rocky promontory, it offered a splendid view over a valley furrowed by a river. It had two towers instead of only one and it was proof of architectural innovation.

Among the many guests gathered in the huge hall of arms, transformed in a reception hall, Godefroy had the happy surprise of meeting a couple of lords, who had come from the Nivernais county. This lord, the count of Epinoy, accompanied by his wife, was a cousin of Othon of Sacht. This is how the baron could inquire about him.

'Othon is very well', answered this cousin,'even if he doesn't own that enthusiasm anymore that you have so admired in him.'

'Ah? What happened to him? He saved my life in the Holy Land and I will never forget it.'

'What?' Continued the cousin, 'do you not know that he has lived the terrible pain of losing his wife, a year ago? He does not leave his home anymore, like he has lost his will to live…'

'By God!' Cried Godefroy. 'Alas, dear sire. I am presently overwhelmed, for I remember his charming wife, so beautiful and sweet! Myself, you see, came alone here, for my wife is very ill and I didn't want her to risk getting cold.'

'How I understand you!' Graciously replied the countess of Epinoy.

Then, chaning tone:

'I am almost certain our cousin would be delighted in seeing you again, for he does not cease to speak of you when he reminisces about the Crusade. I was impressed.'

Lord Lanicey was very flattered.

'So am I', he sincerely declared. 'I would be delighted to see him again, for he has become more than a friend for me: he is a blood brother!'

'In that case', continued the countess, all smiles, 'I will tell him about our encounter here at once.'

'Moreover', added the count of Epinoy, 'I think he would be very honored to receive you in his home. May we tell him you will visit him soon?'

'Well, why not? This will be a very agreeable ride for me, for I love riding through the woods and the countryside.'

'Then allow me to suggest you visit him in a week, the time it would take us to tell him.'

'So be it, I agree. Let's drink to his health!' Declared Godefroy, very happy at the idea of finding his friend again.'

A week later, in the early morning, lord Lanicey galloped at good speed, in the direction of the fortified house of Vauze, on the border of Burgundy, in the Nièvre county.

The earth was so frozen, that it was hard to bury the dead, very numerous that year. They had to burn them on a hill especially arranged for this purpose.

At the entrance of the village, just before the fortress, a man had been left hanging from a tree, and no one had bothered to claim his body. It was probably a poor wretch, without any family.

Godefroy hailed a farmer who was returning his cattle in the stable, and questioned:

'So what did this peasant do, to be condemned thus by the lord here?'

The peasant immediately saw that he was a lord and he answered prudently.

'Bah! - And he wiped the snow encrusted in his long beard – he dared steal wood from the lord of Sacht. If he hadn't been hanged, everyone would have done the same, so this one serves as an example…'

'Indeed', confirmed the baron. 'Your lord is right.'

Without waiting to hear the answer, the man pushed his skinny oxen in the stable, grumbling alone.

The fortified castle appeared after a turn, imposing, isolated from the village that was at its feet. Less big than the fortress of lord Lanicey, compared to an eagle's nest, it emerged in the snowy countryside, very undulating, being built on a hill. It was a rectangular construction, defended by a double row of ditches. Behind the walls was a huge building, flanked by a square tower. This building was surrounded by a belt of machinolations, and topped with a round path. In the first enclosure, there was a church, just like in many villages. The baron thought that it needed to be renovated and thought this fortress less impressive than his own, which was set between rocks. But he admired all the same.

Once announced at the castle, he waited very little in the sitting room, before the door opened to let Othon in, leaping with joy.

«He hasn't changed», remarked lord Lanicey, moved himself. His pleasant face, matte, highlighted by a well maintained mustache, had the same dignity and the same vigor. Just very fine wrinkles appeared at the corners of his blue eyes, witnesses to his recent pain. He hadn't taken on weight and still had a fine look. Godefroy couldn't help but think that his friend could become an ideal catch for his daughter and congratulated himself at this idea.

After sharing a big hug, the two friends observed each other, laughing loudly to mask their emotion. Then Othon took pleasure in presenting him the castle, covered in tapestries on the walls to block the cold. And it was with some pride that he led him to the tower where the top floor was a prison.

41

Godefroy glimpsed a lethal looking cross made of bars to which four men were chained and attached to four huge rings that would have been difficult to break, for the bars were nailed to the ceiling stones. This room was small and round. The walls were extremely thick, measuring around three metres. One sightglass allowed them to see the fields in the distance, currently covered in snow.

'Very good!', he hissed in admiration,' but I have it better: I have dungeons. Are these men enemies?' Godefroy thought of the English.

'Not at all', answered Othon. 'They are simple rebels that must learn obedience here. One always have to gain respect, but I will not teach you this, will I, old brother?'

And he gave him friendly thumps on the back.

Godfrey could only support his claims, he who hesitated not in imprisoning those who had the courage to contradicting him...

Back in the receiving room, which in his wife's time had been a reception room, they drank wine to celebrate their reunion. Then Othon served pure mead with fortifying virtues he had made himself. He also boasted to have tapped physical strength into this brew, a custom he had adopted from the Gauls.

After having swallowed a good number of mugs of perfumed wine, the two friends felt so relaxed that they came to confidences.

'Well, yes', repeated Othon for the umpteenth time, I feel so lonely now, in this castle! I have a few friends like the count of Cravade or lord Griffard fortunately for me, but no one will be able to replace my dear Anne-Claude.'

Godefroy could recognise that his friend was always sad when he had too much wine.

Knowing him fragile in this state, he laughingly suggested:

'Come, my friend! There are not beautiful and wealthy ladies missing in your county. And I suppose that you are of interest to more than one: why not take a second wife? You are younger than me, and at twenty eight, you still look well. And then, did you think you have no heirs?'

'I know. And my poor Anne-Claude could never bring a pregnancy to term… And she suffered greatly.'

The duke sighed deeply and concluded:

'No lady could replace my dear angel, my dear Anne-Claude.'

And he closed his eyes for an instant, to better view her image.

'Not even this one?' Tried the wily baron.

Othon opened his eyes, stunned by this proposal. He then found, completely bewildered, the exquisite drawing of a girl, very young, tended by his friend.

'I present you Lidwine, my daughter', he said with pride. 'Is she not to your liking?'

The brave duke of Sacht remained mute!

He did not know that baron Lanicey had such a pearl of freshness, of natural grace, mixed with a touch of energy, revealed by a sincere, still dreamy look.

Her blond bun, held by a thin veil, conferred her nobility.

Ah! But was he becoming mad? He had trouble tearing his eyes from this bright face!

Then, very quickly, he tried to repress this feeling that had taken him and that otherwise indignated him.

But Godefroy, very sly, detected that instant of failing and, grabbing the right moment, slapped his belly with a big punch before saying.

'Come! Othon, my dear brother in arms, I know what fire your charming wife reign sovereign in your heart, which is absolutely normal. But your life must continue, and you must give an heir to your people. Let's say your second wife will simply be a favourite.'

As the Duke did not answer, he continued.

'I propose you this, that I conceive, may shock you, but it is in all friendship, for your pain hurts to see and I wish to come to your aide. Can you understand this?'

The Duke of Sacht, having come to his senses little by little, could only stammer.

'God! Is it possible?'

'Why not?' added the sire. 'And then, you know well I would be eternally grateful for saving me in the Holy Land, when the Turk wanted to kill me! This is why I think it my duty on my knight's honor to give you my daughter in return. This is what friendship is! Not to mention she will have a good dowry that will allow you to have new lands bordering mine, which will tighten our bonds.'

Was it the effect of the alcohol, which with Othon annihilated his will or altered his judgement? He couldn't say. But this speech had shaken him. He finally managed to answer.

'Listen, I think I would willingly like to try. How could I be able to resist in front of such beauty?'

He remained all shaken, like he had dreamed it…

'May it be at the right time!' Cried Godefroy and served him another glass.

'No, thank you,' answered the last one, ' I had enough to drink for now.'

Othon, having completely found his senses, inquired then.

'But what does your daughter say about this matter?'

Godefroy turned to himself, such a surprise was this question!

'What would you want her to say? She will do what her father will decide for her, like a good daughter.'

'Yes, of course! But I am sentimental, and I would like to have her consent.'

'We will arrange it,' the lord promised, winking at him.

Galloping the other way, the lord congratulated himself for his audacity. His affair had been smoothly conducted! Of course, he had yet to let Lidwine know. And he knew the rebellious character of his daughter. But she was young: he knew well how to persuade her to accept this chance offered her. If not, he would know how to tame her.

Godefroy had gotten rid of his son after Mahaut's emprisonment, for he was too opposing of him, and the baron had to remain the only master of his fortress.

As he had good relations with his overlord, the Duke of Bourgogne, he had agreed with him, before addressing Quentin about perfecting his military education at Dijon for two years. This was the pretext that had been presented to the young man.

Knowing he could not refuse this offer, Quentin had left with a heavy heart for two reasons: on one side, he detested his father's behaviour and on the other side, he had noticed he felt a loving feeling towards Aliénor of Scéry.

This young woman, orphan, and brought by the baron on the death of her father during a fight against the barbarians, was of little nobility and most of all, penniless. Aged eighteen, just like Quentin, he had first considered her a friend, even though she had been pretty even then.

And then the young master had already tried a good number of the women in the village, overturned on a haystack or at the bottom of a barn. But none had left a lasting feeling on him. These had only amused him.

But one day while returning from a hunt, Quentin had inadvertently caught Eleanor bathing in the flowing river below the fortress, in the woods. The young woman, of Spanish origin on her mother's side, had a golden skin. She had untied her long black hair that cascaded to her well-arched posterior. As she had her back to him, he could only see her chest, molded in points when she moved to one side. Thinking she was covered from prying eyes, Aliénor sprayed fresh water and left her hands slide languorously over her intimate forms... For Quentin, she represented a Venus kneaded with pleasure.

The young man had felt love struck, there, at the edge of the river. Then he had slowly climbed off his horse, as to not make a sound and he contemplated her for a long time, his heart beating to get out of his chest. Finally, as her bath had finished, the young woman took her shoes, left by the side, on the ground and donned a long white shirt. Then she approached the castle, seemingly regretful.

Quentin left fifteen days after for Dijon. He had a heavy heart, for he knew that his poor mother hadn't been released, on one hand, and on the other, he had to leave the one he so desired with his body and his heart.

Fourth part

The next day after this successful encounter with his friend, lord Lanicey sent for his daughter. He was in the room that contained the archives of the fortress, as well as different plans and tomes. Situated at the last floor of the tower, it constituted a place for private meeting, away from prying ears. It was reached by a screw staircase carved into thick walls. A guard surveyed the access. It was there he gathered his comrades in arms, if need be: he had summoned them to preach to the formerly on the need to combat the infidels. It was there he made plans for a battle or organized a strategy to drive back the enemy.

He had chosen this room to meet with Lidwine with the intention of intimidating her. The young woman knew of the existence of this room, but she had rarely come, except for visits, for in principle, ladies were excluded.

Godefroy was thus telling her it was an honor.

Inviting his daughter to sit, he contemplated with rapture her beauty, resembling that of her mother in the past. He had married Mahaut when she had been fifteen, older than Lidwine, and this marriage had been chosen by him. For Mahaut, he had melted with love! In his view, he had felt his blood boil in all senses and he had only thought of his wedding night who had come too slow, in his taste. In that time, the unending wars that ravaged the countries hadn't mattered at all for him. He was pinning for his bride: but he was just a man!

'Lidwine', he began in a firm tone, ' I made you come here for a serious reason. I have a plan for you, me, your father who loves and honors you, like you well know. I have already made allusions of this plan repeatedly, but my decision wasn't certain. Or, it is so at present.'

Lidwine, sensing a grave moment, baring in mind the place where she had been summoned, wisely remained seated without moving. Only her long eyelashes fluttered against her eyelids, indicating she was still alive. Strongly intrigued, she doubted her father had engineered something in her regard, but she was determined not to give in too fast to his wishes.

'Look!' He said with an important air, 'what I wish is for you own good: you are reaching an age when a young girl of your rang can think of taking a husband, to make the happiness of a gentleman of value, a good warrior, moreover who will know to watch over you. Life is short and my years are numbered at present. My duty is to ensure your future by your marriage with a man worthy of you.'

Hearing these words, Lidwine couldn't help but start.

« God! she thought, who will he find as my suitor? » Since a while, her heart moved tenderly only in the presence of Guillame, a young valet or a page the Duke of Lorraine had placed with her father in order for him to teach the art of war. This young man began devouring her with his eyes since a year ago. In the beginning, Lidwine hadn't paid any attention, considering him a playmate, for he had become the friend of her brother, Quentin. Then, one day when she was trying to observe her image, leaning above the well, where the water referred the reflection of her delicate face, framed by blond braids, she noticed Guillame's gaze upon her, and she could read the admiration he felt for her.

Lidwine had kept this sweet secret for herself, afraid of losing it if she revealed it to anyone. She came out of her musings when the baron said:

'It is so that I have thought of uniting you with a valiant knight, an old friend, since we fought together in the same Crusade. He is older than you, for certain, but he has courage and kindness.'

'Oh Father!', she energetically answered, 'I do not doubt your good intention in my concern, and I thank you. But, please, keep me under your roof a little longer: I am in no haste to marry.'

'And why is that?', said the lord, amazed.

'Well, because I do not feel I am ready… and then…'

Guillame's existence wasn't the only cause for the lack of eagerness.

She took a firm tone of her own:

'Father, you must know that I will not leave this home as long as my mother will remain captive in a horrible dungeon. It is inconceivable to me!'

Lidwine lifted her chin insolently and didn't turn her eyes away from the lightnings of fury that came from the lord.

She knew that was the only argument that counted more than any other if she was to stop her father's decision.

Lord Lanicey furrowed his thick eyebrows similar to the mane of a horse, they were so long, and with a strong voice thundered:

'Never! Do you hear me? That bitch doesn't exist anymore.'

Then he went on.

'Excuse my expression in designated the one who was once your mother.'

Lidwine, used to her father's outbursts, didn't let herself be intimidated. Unlike lady Mahaut, her venerable mother, she hid an iron hand in a velvet glove.

'But, Father', she tried to respond by trying to conceal her anger, 'I do not wish to refuse this plan at the moment: I am simply asking your agreement to stay with her, knowing her under these stones.'

Godefroy hadn't thought about this situation, that counteracted his plans. He kept walking in the room trying to calm down and try to think. He knew his daughter well enough, as well as her stubbornness, of which he was proud, for it showed her belonging to his glorious ancestors. But he would break this will at need, for, after all, her sex aside, she had to submit.

Furious, he made a gesture in the direction of the door, which signified that she could retire. But Lidwine didn't take it so. Her curiosity took her:

'May I least know the name of the one you wish to tie my fate to?'

The lord mellowed a little.

'Yes, it's about the Duke Othon of Sacht, twenty eight years of age. It is thanks to his zeal I am still alive. He is a widow of a year and mourns the fact he has no heirs. He is a very handsome man, believe me, and endowed with a wonderful heart. He has a beautiful fortress in the Nivernais county.'

'Then allow me to be surprised. How come he hasn't found a lady to suit his taste?'

'Because he is demanding and does not wish to marry a silly girl who will throw herself at him, coveting his property.'

He especially insisted upon the fact that his friend didn't seem hostile at the prospect of marriage, omitting however, to reveal that he had shown him her portrait. And he supported the fact that she will become a duchess, an important honor, of course.

In the days following this meeting, Lidwine tried not to find herself in the presence of her father, alone. Fortunately, their meals were taken with everyone, with Aliénor, whom she considered a sister. She, to whom she had confided all her concerns, was quite indecisive: on one hand, she understood well the baron's worries in the face of tomorrow's uncertainties. But on the other hand, she shared Lidwine's revolt concerning the awful, unjust fate lived by her mother.

'Listen', Aliénor advised her, a day when the lord had decided to meet the steward to make the stock revenues of the fields, 'nothing obliges you to give your answer so soon. You are young and you can ask for the benefit of reflection. Therefore, you will appear more wise...'

Lidwine was on the point of confiding her sweet secret regarding Guillaume, then she thought better, thinking that maybe, it was premature.

Godefroy received a messenger from his friend, the Duke, charged with transmitting that after careful consideration, he accepted the marriage proposition with Lidwine. This would allow him, with her dowry, to begin the renovation of his fortress. But he did not dare admit that he already found himself under the charms of this young beauty.

The lord thought about Lidwine's decision, knowing that she wanted her mother's return among them before marrying, and he realized it was indispensable to make Mahaut disappear for this marriage to take place. For him, she had been dead for a long time.

He inquired the guards about her state of health and they informed him that she was barely alive... Then it would be very easy to cut her life forever.

To do this, he sent for Ulric, the servant of his heart, in his secret room, found in the high dungeon, and ordered him these:

'Dear friend, I need a pretty special favour from you, and I truly think you are the only one I trust.'

'I am very flattered, my lord', answered the terrible henchman. And his face of weathered and hard features lit up with a smile of satisfaction.

'What I want to ask requires extreme prudence and most of all, absolute secrecy.'

Godefroy cleared his voice a little, and then said at once:

'Look! It's about you ending Mahaut's life, this bitch who ruined my reputation and my supremacy in this fortress. But everyone must think she died naturally.'

Ulric didn't even blink and made a bow in front of his master before saying:

'It will be done as you wish, master and lord! By I will need a key in order to enter her dungeon.'

'This is not even a problem: I will get you one. But remember what I told you. Only you and I know the truth.'

'You have nothing to fear', repeated that man without heart. 'When would I make my move?'

'The sooner the better. Why not this night, while everyone is asleep?'

The lord searched in a secret drawer of his work table and took out a key for Ulric.

'Here, I give it in your care, but report to me tomorrow morning, after your task is completed. I will be in this room. Come, good luck!'

When the night was advanced and all the inhabitants of the fortress were sleeping, a shadow slipped into the tunnel that led to the dungeons. Mahaut's guard having been sufficiently drunk to not wake up, a man went into the interior of the prison. He barely looked at the baroness who was only a small cluster of bones, topped with a shock of white hair. You would have said she was already gone from this world! However, she was still feebly breathing. The man grabbed the blanket that covered her, rolled it into a ball and stuck it for a long time on Mahaut's face. She struggled very little and her last breath was stifled by the blanket... After having assured himself that she was really dead, the man, indifferent before this spectacle, put the old cover to its place. Then he ran away very softly by another underground passage which gave access to the outside, along the ramparts.

The next morning, Ulric presented himself before his master, already busy in his study. He just gave him the secret key and said, his mouth twisted by an evil grin:

'Job done!'

Godefroy let a sigh of relief escape him.

'Very well! And remember one thing: if you betray this secret, you will be hanged!'

'Do not worry, sire. In exchange, what will I receive as reward? For a job like this is worth some gratification.'

The lord thought for a brief moment, then answered.

'I name you superintendent of this fortress. And you will report all those who behave badly.'

'This suits me just perfectly and I thank you.'

Then the baron pointed to the door, for certain servants woke up early.

A little while after that, Mahaut's bodyguard informed him of the prisoner's death, which did not affect Godefroy's mood.

'It's just as well!' He confessed. 'She was too weak.'

'What should I do with her body?' Asked the guard.

'Bury her beneath the big oak. But hurry, for the sun will soon rise. And no one must see her.'

Soon, news of the death of the one who at once, had shined of beauty, spread like a trail of powder. Many servants began to cry for her. Hildegarde, Lidwine and Quentin's old nurse, began crying bitter tears and retired to her room to hide her pain: she had guessed the lord had been her assassin, locking her until her death in a sombre dungeon. But she kept this thought to herself. When Lidwine found out about her mother's death, she gave a long cry of pain and refused to go down for breakfast and other meals, not being able to stand sitting next to her father. She locked herself in her room by pushing a piece of furniture before the door and refused to leave, not opening but to her friend Aliénor. But she was not successful in consoling her.

She brought meals that Lidwine pushed away with rage, indicating by this that she would rather die...

Around the end of a week, Lidwine recognized her father's heavy footsteps coming towards her room. He violently rapped on the door, then thrust it with a kick of his shoulder.

'Hey Lidwine!' He screamed. 'When will you stop this lamentable comedy? You are not worthy of your father, of your ancestors.'

But the young girl hid under her cover, saying nothing.

The lord, under the influence of anger, threatened her in these words:

'If you do not present yourself in the kitchen, I will drag you by force! Do you understand?'

Then Lidwine got up and with insolence, passed before her father, throwing at his face:

'You are nothing but an assassin!'

At these words, the lord slapped her with all his might.

Lidwine became livid, but she understood that the baron remained the strongest. So she went to eat, taking care not to look at her father. At the end of the meal, Aliénor took her for a walk in the fields.

Summer having come to an end, a great party was organized by the lord of Lanicey, like every year, at the end of harvesting.

For this, Lidwine made the effort to leave the fortress, conscious she had the duty to show herself to the village inhabitants.

Everywhere, flowers decorated the cottages, even the most miserable ones. They were only sparks of roses, white lilies and gold, intermingled with daisies, cornflowers and poppies brought from the fields by the young women in the village. The merchants and barkers had the opportunity to

54

spread on boards, supported by trestles, various objects of interest: toys made and sculpted in wood that made the children's eyes sparkle; perfumes smelling of musk and cinnamon, brought back by the Crusaders, and having the power, it was said, to make one fall in love; light and vaporous fabrics for amorous encounters. Indeed, many lords had been invited to this party, and were accompanied, some by their wives, some by their mistresses. These dressed in their best outfits and wore beautiful jewelry.

Acrobats were performing thousands of feats to impress the onlookers. Everywhere, cries and laughter abounded. Accompanied by Hildegarde, her old nurse that served as a chaperone - she had breastfed not less than sixteen children – Lidwine began to sigh. Sometimes she envied the simple young women, peasants or servants, who could take advantage of their freedom, when they were not yet married.

She noticed her father busy gesticulating, surrounded by a small group of knights:

«They talk of war, no doubt? » She thought, and this annoyed her to no end.

Suddenly, a gentleman bowed before her, hat in hand and said:

'May I offer you this bouquet?'

Surprised, she could only answer.

'I can not refuse, sire, but with whom do I have the honor?'

'My name is of no importance. What counts, for me, is that you accept it, and this will make me happy.' This man, who had a way with words, didn't lack assurance, which flattered her despite herself.

Intrigued by this mysterious character, Lidwine looked at him more closely: he was not even ugly! His demeanour emanated force, and a little bit of sweetness appeared on this face lightly accentuated by time. But she wouldn't have known what age to give him.

To escape, Lidwine took the bouquet, gratified the stranger with a charming smile in acknowledgment and continued on her way.

Hildegarde told her:

'This gentleman remarked you, and this is a good thing. No doubt he fell in love with you?'

'This would surprise me, dear Hilda' – diminutive of Hildgarde – 'for he does not know me at all...'

In the evening, at the castle, among the guests who were moving and drank with gusto, she recognised that admirative face. But the gentleman did not leave his place, which she appreciated.

The lord of Lanicey let several days pass before making another appointment ment with his daughter. After installing her on the stern seat that suited the warriors, between those thick walls that guarded all secrets, he questioned her with a playful air.

'Then, my dear daughter, how did you feel about your meeting with lord Sacht? Tell me everything.'

She could not help herself being startled, then indignant.

'Come, father, you are not serious, I assume? I did not meet your friend, happily for him.'

'Are you truly certain?' He answered with a predatory smile, for it did not reveal but the right side of his moustache.

'Absolutely certain. Unless...'

She remembered the unknown gentleman's gesture who had dared offer her a bouquet. Lidwine suddenly understood why he had not revealed his name. Was it possible it had been him? Becoming pale, she remained thoughtful for a short moment...

'Unless what?' Repeated the lord with a false, easygoing tone, but which let a small point of triumph be seen.

She remained obstinate nonetheless.

'If I tell you I haven't seen him! Else, you would have introduced him to me, following the usages of this world that you can not ignore.'

'As a matter of fact, I had no need to introduce him to you', he bellowed laughing, 'for he told me he put himself at your service, and he thought he understood you did not refuse him.'

This time, no doubt was possible. She regretted her foolishness.

'What?' She said in her turn. 'Thus, you have played me. He disgusts me, as you do as well.'

The young woman got up, caught with fury, and barely restrained herself in imitating her father, who threw whatever he found in his way in cases such as this one.

'Enough!' She said while getting up. 'But I warn you that this does not tie me to this man at all.'

The lord managed to hide his wrath.

'This is where you are wrong, dear child, but, believe me, you will not regret it, for this friend is charming.'

'I will not do your unfaithful tricks, not worthy of a gentleman', she cried, exasperated.

'Your opinions are of not importance in this matter. It is my choice and I stand by it!' He added, hitting his fist on the table.

His face had become red with fury.

'Now', he told her, 'you may retire.'

Lidwine left, furious. In her blue eyes, black flames shined.

She left in search of Aliénor, her greatest confidante and friend. She was just coming back from the garden and immediately noticed Lidwine's frowning face.

'What is happening, little sister?' She affectionately asked.

The young girl told her about her encounter with her father, and the way he had mocked her about her marriage with the duke.

Aliénor listened in silence, then made her think.

'Unfortunately I now that your father is capable of worse facts. But in what concerns his friend, what shows you that he is not sincere?'

'Oh, come on!' exclaimed Lidwine, 'for me it is evident that he had an understanding with my father, before the party.'

'And even if he had, who is it to say he has no feelings for you?'

Lidwine then remembered the scene that took place during the party, in the course of which the duke had offered her flowers, and she smiled.

'Maybe you are right.'

'On the other hand', said Aliénor, 'I think that you will feel safer next to a man who has already lived and suffered.'

'Ah! How I envy your wisdom!' Revealed Lidwine. 'You are always such a good counsel to me, and I thank you. Then I will marry this man, but I will let my father understand that I have not obeyed him. It is because this gentleman seduced me.'

The marriage was celebrated as a grand affair a month later. All the neighboring nobility was invited. The festivities lasted for a week. Finally Otho, radiant, could welcome his pretty wife like a princess in his fortress.

Then came a day when, feeling lonely, not having anyone to contradict with, the lord thought of Quentin. He made a request to his sovereign, inquiring after his son's military skills. Then duke of Bourgogne wasn't late in bringing praise to this young warrior, mastering all battle techniques, making him happy.

The lord was greatly flattered and the idea came to write to his son in these words:

«My dear son,

I have heard from high places of your warrior exploits, which make me very satisfied. And it is the reason why I decided to make you come back to our lands. Do not forget that you are my only son, heir to the Lanicey fortress, and that it is your duty to succeed me, now that the years are passing. We are always afraid of invaders, especially since the king of the Franks tries to conquer our county.

I will await your positive answer in all haste.

Your honorable father. »

When Quentin received this missive, he became pale and aghast.

'What happened?' Asked his best friend, Roland of Chessac. ' Are you upset with your love? Still, all the pretty ladies in Dijon and its surroundings swoon before you.'

'No, it's worse than this! I have just received a letter from my father ordering me to go back to our lands, and this does not make me happy at all.'

'How I understand you!' comiserated Roland. 'Especially since you ravage female hearts.'

'This may be true, but it is of little importance. I do not feel ready for marriage.'

'Then maybe you already love someone?'

Quentin thought of Aliénor, whose wonderful image hadn't stopped haunting him during these two years. But he preferred to keep his silence, not being certain that this love was shared.

'Did you notice that the beautiful Aglaé of La Rocherie has eyes only for you?' Continued his friend.

'Yes, I find Aglaé charming, but not to a big extent.'

'Will you go to the ball organized tomorrow evening at the duke of Bourgogne's?'

'Yes', answered Quentin. 'I can't refuse this invitation, it would be impolite.'

'This is good, for I will be going as well!' Declared Roland.

The next evening, the two friends had their best attire on and presented themselves to the ball.

The noble ladies wore splendid dresses, and their jewelry shined under the lights. A good number of ladies hoped to find the future elected of their heart ...

When the dances began in a huge room prepared for this occasion, Aglaé quickly came to Quentin's side, who could not refuse her. The two friends, not only good warriors, were also excellent dancers. Abruptly, in the middle of the dance, Aglaé was seized with a sudden discomfort, for she collapsed into the arms of the young man who held her to prevent her from falling.

This did not escape her father's sharp eye, the marquis of La Rocherie, who immediately advanced to Quentin, and told him as follows:

'Excuse me, dear sir, for bothering you. But your attitude while dancing with my daughter hasn't escaped me. I think you are dishonoring Aglaé in keeping her in your arms, in the eyes of all and due to this fact, you must marry her.'

Quentin, completely dazed, tried to defend himself.

'Marquis, I admit you are making me a great honor in proposing the hand of your daughter, but I have not dishonored her at all. It is her who remained attached to my arm.'

'It is as I have said! And your marriage will repair your actions.'

'I am sincerely sorry', answered the young man,' but this marriage is not conceivable.'

'And why not?' Replied the marquis.

'Because my father asks me to go back to our ancestral lands as soon as possible.'

'And what of it? I do not see where the problem is? Aglaé will follow you there.'

'Dear marquis, I am afraid she will be extremely bored there, lost in the forest. Not to mention the hard winters in this country clinging to the banks of the Jura mountains.'

But the marquis didn't want to hear anything else. Then Quentin thought that he had to find an irrefutable argument.

'Must I remind you, lord la Rocherie, that I am a simple baron and I think Aglaé would be happier with a gentleman of a superior rank. She can afford to marry a count, or even a duke!'

The marquis thought for a moment, then said:

'What you say is true. Then, I ask you to excuse me for bothering you.'

Quentin, having found his good humor, made a bow and answered:

'But believe me, you are excused.'

The marquis took a look in the room and saw that, indeed, Aglaé, was abandoning herself, with delight, in the arms of a fortunate young count.

Then Quentin turned to his friend Roland.

'Come, it is too hot here!'

'If I had been in your place, I would have accepted to marry Aglaé', said Roland.

'There is nothing stopping you to ask for her hand, since you are a count.'

'It is what I will try to do at the next ball.'

And they went back to their lodgings, smiling.

Back in his room, Quentin took a piece of paper, a quill pen and ink to answer his father.

« Dearest father,
Your letter moved me and I share your point of view regarding the Franks and we must hold them back. But allow me to answer that I wish to enroll in our emperor's army, for better battling them. I hope you understand my decision, which is well thought upon.
Your faithful son. »

Quentin immediately summoned a messenger to inform baron Lanicey of this decision. It didn't matter his father would be angry after reading the letter. But he had to know!

During these two years, his character had shown, battling others. He wanted to show him he could take care of himself, and that he wasn't a son who was completely submissive.

But the following week, he received a menacing answer from the baron.

« *My son,*

If you will dishonor me by refusing to come to Lanicey, I will have no choice but to disinherit you, in favor of the child that your sister, married to the duke of Sacht is now carrying. Then you will remain the simple soldier you wish to become.

Godefroy of Lanicey »

Despite his anger, Quentin had to obey this irrefutable *order*. In fact, he did not want to be a simple soldier, always having to follow his superiors' orders.

Further, Aliénor's image taking her bath in the river had never ceased to haunt him…

When he glimpsed the fortress, crossing the forest, he felt moved, for a flow of memories invaded him.

He understood then that his place must be there, in this recessed stronghold among the mountains. He slowly skirted the river in the foolish hope of seeing Aliénor, but the young girl wasn't bathing.

Arriving, all the servants ran to meet him, happy to see him among them again. Quentin searched Aliénor with his eyes, but he did not find her.

'Ah! Look how beautiful and strong you have become!' Exclaimed old Hildegarde, drying her tears of joy.

Indeed, under his blond hair, reaching his collar, his black eyes made a startling contrast. His shoulders were wider and a certain silent force emanated from his person.

'And how happy I am to hug you!' Answered Quentin, hugging her to him.

He shortly told her what he had lived in Dijon. But since having found his native home, an idea obsessed him. In the end, he dared ask.

'And my mother, tell me, what has become of her?'

The consternation, then the tears of the old nurse, made him understand that his mother was no more…

Quentin dropped into a chair, prey to a vivid despair that he did not succeed in masking, even though he was a man, and they had to remain masters of their feelings.

Hilda stopped her cries and made to serve him a comforting liqueur. But Quentin thought, as well:

«My father killed her!» And a feeling of hate invaded his pained heart.

Betrand, the young page employed by the lord after Guillame's departure, bade him a friendly welcome.

'I am very happy to finally meet you, sire', he said. 'I have heard a lot of praises about you, and I do not want to hide the fact I wish to resemble you.'

'I deeply thank you for this warm welcome and you have my friendship. Do not hesitate to consult me in case of trouble. I will always be here for you.'

Then, the young baron followed his duty to present himself before his father. He climbed directly to his study, in the high tower, being certain of finding him there.

The lord, on his side, had already seen his son cross the drawbridges, but he did not move, thinking his son had to make the first step.

'Enter!' He said in a rough voice when he struck against the oak door.

Quentin entered and stood dumbfounded for a moment: he had expected to find his father aged at the end of these two years. It was what the lord had left to understand in his message. But, to his great surprise, he saw him in very good shape for his forty years. His hair had not whitened, his skin was tanned by the sun had very little deep wrinkles, apart from those surrounding his lips, slightly limp on the sides, for he was not missing many teeth. Only his thick eyebrows and beard were interspersed with white hair.

His tall stature always imposed respect, but Quentin now surpassed him.

Godefroy, on his side, greatly admired his heir, who emanated force and beauty, and he felt a sliver of jealousy.

Fifth part

'Sit down, my son. You have become a man, and you will be ready to second me in my work.'

'What is it that you expect from me, father?' Asked Quentin, seated in front of him.

'You will wake up very early each morning, you will check if the guards are well at their posts. Then you will leave for the villages in order to survey if the villagers do their jobs well.'

Quentin jumped in his seat, suddenly annoyed.

'But it is for this you made me come back? I was expecting a more noble undertaking. You are simply proposing me the role of guardian, when I have studied the art of war.'

And his cheeks colored with indignation.

'But', replied the sire, 'it will be you who will battle the attackers who are always in the area. You will be more efficient than me, I have no doubt.'

'So', followed the young man, 'you will still be the indisputable master of this fortress?'

'Obviously! Until my death, which I hope will be long in coming.'

Quentin got up without his father's permission to take leave of him, as he felt nauseated. But the lord signaled the order to stay.

'You are in a hurry to leave, my son. Wait until you find out what I have planned for your good.'

The young man resumed his seat, sighing.

«What does he still want from me?» When his father was concerned, he could expect anything.

The sire announced in an important tone:

'I have in plan to marry you to our neighbor, the marquis's daughter, Bertille of Attrans.'

'Oh, no, father, there is no question of that!'

'And why not?' Replied the lord, surprised and annoyed.

'Have you already seen her? She has a pimpled face and her body is already overweight.'

The lord hunched his shoulders.

'So what? This is will not prevent her from giving you beautiful children.'

But Quentin insisted.

'Anyway, since you must know, in fact I love Aliénor of Scéry.'

Godfrey remained speechless. But he persisted.

'You will marry Bertille, for you owe me obedience, that is all.'

Quentin, beside himself, got up from his seat to take his leave. Then he went for a walk in the countryside to calm himself.

That evening, Quentin didn't manage to sleep, he was so agitated! However, his long journey had tired him. He had to, at all costs, meet Aliénor to declare his love, for her bright image almost made him suffer.

During the night, he made plans in his fevered head, sometimes ridiculous, sometimes foolish. Then he plunged, harassed in a dreamless sleep.

The next morning, after waking up fairly late, Quentin left directly in the direction of the villages, like his father had ordered.

At half way, going to the woods, a shaft fed water to the fortress, and it was Aliénor who would draw water that day. When he arrived near her, a breath of love invaded him.

The young woman remained leaning over the well, like searching for something.

She got up soon to make him her best bow, but Quentin stopped her.

'Come, Aliénor, do not bow to me: we have known each other for so long!'

'It is true, but you are still a lord.'

'That aside, tell me what you are doing, leaning over this well.'

Aliénor sighed deeply.

'I am looking for my ring that fell into this well. And I am most unhappy, for it belonged to my poor mother. It was the only object I had left of her…'

And tears moistened her ember, beautiful eyes.

Moved, Quentin hurried to say:

'Do not worry. I can offer you a better one, decorated with a diamond.'

Aliénor raised her head, stupefied.

'But why would I deserve such a beautiful gift?'

Then, the young baron took a deep breath and confessed:

'It's because… since two years ago… I burn with love for you. Since I have left for Dijon, not one single day has passed… without thinking of you. You are so beautiful!'

Still, he dared not confess that he had surprised her while bathing nude in the river, just before his departure.

He continued with fervor.

'Aliénor, I wish to marry you. Could you fall in love with me?'

'Oh, lord! How could I refuse, me, who am but a poor orphan, penniless and of little nobility?'

'But you are my princess, my goddess…'

And saying this, Quentin hugged her to him and placed very soft kisses on her shiny hair. At this contact, he felt her tremor of pleasure…

Then, in her turn, Aliénor said:

'Oh! If you only knew, Quentin! I have loved you since your father first brought me here…'

Then, in the same spirit, their lips met.

'Yes', she repeated, 'I will be your wife for life.'

Then, suddenly, leaving space for reality, Aliénor had to break the magic by asking:

'But what will your father say? Do you think he will approve of our union? Maybe he wishes you to marry a lady of higher rank than mine?'

Quentin shook his head and said in a form voice:

'If my father is opposed to our union, I will leave him.'

'Oh, no!' Cried the young girl. 'I beg you not to leave me, now that we love each other.'

'Do not fear, my adored one, I will not leave you.'

Then he kissed her passionately to seal these words.

'Nonetheless', he continued, 'I think we must remain prudent, in order not to raise his fury.'

They embraced each other one last time and then, with regret, Quentin went down to the village.

During two months, the two young lovers could find themselves in the fields, under the summer's sun, without being bothered. Quentin burned with the desire to rid her of her clothes and to merge with her. Her flesh was so appetizing! But Aliénor, steeped in religion, always refused to give him her body. And Quentin, because he was so in love with her, did not want to rush her.

It was Hildegarde who served as intermediary, happy to be of service to the one she cherished as her own son. Her husband, Waldemar, had extinguished shortly after Mahaut's death, like he couldn't take this loss. And after Lidwine's departure, her ray of sunshine, she felt void. Thanks to Quentin's return, she lived again.

When the baron of Lanicey was out of the fortress to visit his friend or to castigate his peasants, she was quick to warn them. And the two lovebirds went away quietly in nature…

Until one day when he saw their looks during a meal. Godefroy pretended not to have seen anything, but he thought: «Damn it, these two are in love!» and jealousy began to form in him, in addition to a strong annoyance, for he wished his son to marry Bertille.

He swore to find a vengeance worthy of him.

Finding nothing by himself, he called for Ulric, whose imagination was rich enough to satisfy evil inclinations.

Godefroy summoned him, as usual, in his study, in the high tower.

'What can I do for you, master?'

'I would love for you to give me an idea for a vengeance concerning my son.'

He explained his marriage project between Quentin and Bertille of Attrans, plan which would fail, for his son had fallen for Aliénor.

And this is what that unscrupulous man got out from his malignant brain:

'I have an idea, sire, but I do not know if it will be convenient for you.'

'Still, tell it. Do not fear. It is only us two here!'

The face of the terrible henchman flourished with evil joy.

'Well, it will be enough for you to ask the hand in marriage of this damsel. As she is indebted to you for everything, she will no doubt, dare refuse you. And this is how Quentin will have no choice but to marry the one you have chosen for him.'

Godefroy felt really exhilarated at this idea, for if he had never trussed Aliénor, in memory of his father, this desire had suddenly come!

The lord burst with laughter.

'Ulric, you are a true genius! This idea suits me perfectly, for this young girl is a beautiful chick that I will still be able to honor. I feel completely capable!'

'Then, may it be at the right time!' Exclaimed Ulric proudly, whose face disfigured when he laughed more.

In fact, his small, lewd eyes disappeared under a mountain of wrinkles, and his mouth, usually slumped, rose to his hairy ears.

'Yes, that's it!' Godefroy added, all pleased. 'Let's drink together to my remarriage.'

He got up and took out of a secret panel a good bottle of very strong liqueur, the same one which he had offered to the unfortunate street vendors that had crossed the valley. Only it did not contain poison.

Godefroy made sure once again of the complete discretion of this henchman, and this one assured him entirely.

'Come, master, you can trust me. Have you heard anyone complain about Mahaut's assassination?'

'No! No one made this remark and happily for them, as I would have killed him.'

'Then let us drink to your remarriage!'

The two accomplices started laughing so much that one of the guards came after them.

'We heard noise, that is why we came', explained one of them.

'Quickly return to your post!' Screamed the lord. 'This does not concern you.'

Two days later, the lord called for Quentin, the meeting to be still in his study. Quentin was wondering why his father wanted to see him again.

'Sit down, dear son, I must tell you something about me.'

Quentin was surprised and worried.

'What is happening, father?'

'I must think about my old age.'

'Why? Are you ill?'

'No. During my whole life I have fought, I have traveled across the world, especially in the third Crusade, that almost cost me my life. And now, I want my days to be more peaceful.'

'I am relieved, father! Have you become more wise?'

The cunning sire laughed under his breath.

'To tell you the truth, no. I imagine my future near a sweet and faithful companion, who will brighten my old days.'

Quentin twitched in his chair.

'Father! Have you gone mad? How dare you speak like this when you have made my mother suffer locking her in a dungeon?'

'Let us not go back to the past. What has been done doesn't interest us anymore. It is best to concentrate especially on the present and future. And then, I have changed during the years... Now, I feel capable of bringing lots of love to the one who will brighten my last days.'

Quentin thought he had gone mad.

'How can you speak of love? This feeling does not exist in you.'

But the sire banged his fist on the table.

'And how dare you judge me? Since when do children allow themselves to command their ancestors? I will do as I see fit, even if this does not suit you.'

The young man understood he had gone too far and calmed himself.

'Then', he said, 'may I know the name of the one, I am certain, will be most unhappy?'

'Oh, yes! You already know her, anyway: it is Aliénor of Scéry.'

Quentin felt like the sky had fallen on him. Then he rushed to his father, with the desire to wring his neck. But a table separated them, and the sire had retreated.

'Father! I forbid you to marry Aliénor, for it is I whom she loves.'

'Are you truly certain?' Sneered the latter. 'Maybe she will change her mind, for she will become the richest woman in our county. I will cover her in gold and her beauty will be highlighted.'

'But I love her and she loves me, I tell you!'

The lord merely shrugged his broad shoulders.

'Oh, yes? And what do you know of love? You are so young and inexperienced!'

Quentin, nauseated, exclaimed:

'Father, know I will not take your insults. And I ask retribution. For this, we must organize a battle between the two of us.'

'Willingly!' Answered Godefroy. 'You do not impress me at all. For I have fought so much during my life! Then I will meet you tomorrow morning, at dawn, at the edge of the woods. We will not need witnesses.'

'I will be there.'

In a rage, Quentin overthrew his chair. Then, without looking at his father, he slipped outside, to breathe the clean and soothing air of the country.

The next morning, at dawn, dew covered the herbs, as well as the trees, who had started to lose their leaves. Autumn pointed its nose with its procession of mists and days becoming lighter in color. The air had become more crisp.

Seated on a tree trunk, Quentin was waiting for his father. He knew the latter would make him wait. He had grabbed, a club by chance, refusing to use a weapon against his own father. For, if he was his rival, the lord remained, nonetheless, his father. Finally, Godefroy appeared with empty hands as well. If Quentin had the force and the boldness of youth, the lord felt animated by hatred. Then, all of sudden, he threw himself on his son, while saying a string of expletives, and stuffed punches in his ribs.

Quentin responded by hitting his club against his father's legs, trying to make him fall. But the lord avoided this jumping aside, then, driven by unspeakable anger, took a huge rock and launched it flying in the direction of his son. Quentin barely had time to avoid it, but the rock had touched his forehead. A trail of blood, mixed with his sweat, dripped on his lips. He thought that Aliénor ignored this battle and that she would be frightened if he went back hurt.

Then, he raised his arm signaling that he ended this ridiculous battle. The lord, all out of breath, accepted the truce and said, all proud:

'Go take care of your wound. It is only superficial.'

Then the two men went their separate ways, for the day was advancing.

So, Godefroy had the feeling of having defeated his son, and a feeling of pride invaded him.

At the beginning of the afternoon, as had been arranged, Aliénor, went at the foot of an oak, where the lovers had the habit to meet. But curiously, Quentin didn't show himself.

It was the first time he missed this meeting. After having waited for him for an hours, she went back to the fortress, worried. What had happened to her love?

She questioned Hildegarde, who knew nothing. Then, she resumed her job of clerk, hoping to see him at dinner. Not for a moment did she doubt his love for her. She was sure of the feelings that united them. However, she remained worried until dinner time, when she didn't see him come.

'Do you know where Quentin is?' She ingenuously asked the sire.

'My word, I know nothing.' he calmly answered.

Aliénor becoming sad, had not appetite and contented herself to push the food around her plate.

As she was feeling weary, the young girl decided to go back to her room earlier than usual. She was not sleepy, but she laid on her bed. The weather was stormy, the wind blew in the high firs, and it was really dark in the chamber. She shed her clothes and put on her long white shirt.

Aliénor was on the verge of sleeping when she suddenly heard footstep on the wooden stairs that led to her room. Who could come? For a moment, she hoped it was Quentin, but she didn't recognize his walk. The wood creaked under the weight of boots! Or, only the baron wore boots here.

Beside herself, she felt a tremor of fear traveling the length of her spine. In one leap, she rose to save herself in time.

But already a big hand grabbed her by the arm and pushed her back in the room.

The lord – for it was really him – approached her saying:

'Come here, my chick, for I have come to honor you before our marriage that will take place soon.'

And he let out a guttural laugh while watching her lustfully. He had coveted her for so long!

'No! Leave me alone!' Cried the young girl crying. She stepped back as far as she could while calling.

'Hilda! Hilda! Help! Help me!'

But the lord kept laughing.

'It is useless to call Hilda. I have sent her to her daughter's until tomorrow... We will not be bothered...'

Aliénor began screaming in terror, but in vain. Of a sudden gesture, he tore her shirt from top to bottom, and could admire her tempting curves. He grabbed a breast like he would pick a fruit. It was elastic and firm at the same time, which excited him more.

Aliénor begged him.

'Let me go! You are hurting me!'

'No! Let yourself go, my darling, if not, I will break both of them, which would be a pity...'

In that moment, a sudden lightning illuminated the room, then thunder began violently. But Godefroy, felt electrified by the storm, like it was giving him its force and determination.

He grabbed her other breast and drew her to him. He had the impression of grasping two beautiful apples, tasty to eat. Then he pushed her on her bed. He crushed her with all his weight, while his large mouth descended on Aliénor's, like an enormous slimy vacuum. Understanding she was lost, the young girl didn't resist anymore. She even wished he would his dirty work finish sooner! She began to weep silently while, with his big fingers, he spread her slender thighs and tore her sweet intimacy...

Then, with a violent assault, he possessed her, pushing with a cry of pleasure like the roar of a lion.

When he finished his crime, he watched her one last time: she remained completely immobile, even though she suffered greatly. Only tears flooded her contorted face and streamed down her magnificent matted hair.

Thinking she had fallen asleep, he retired and went away, satisfied with himself. Henceforth, Aliénor belonged to him.

Quentin woke early to go the closest village, the next morning of his ridiculous battle against his father. He wanted to keep this wretched memory a secret, so he would not frighten his love. He did not want her to see his light wound on the forehead. That is why he had avoided showing himself at dinner the other night.

Suddenly, at his back, he heard a voice calling him.

'Quentin! Help! Quentin!'

He turned and saw a distant figure that waved while running. Great was his surprise when he recognised Aliénor, dressed in haste, and carrying a meager bundle!

When she reached him, she slumped in his arms, crying.

'My darling, my adored one, what has happened to you? Are you ill?'

The young girl nodded her head, but still, could not say a word.

Quentin hugged her strongly, and kissed her everywhere on her face filled with tears.

At the end of a long moment, she was able to recover her breath and said:

'It is the lord… he has… he has…'

And then she began to cry.

Quentin then thought he understood everything.

'He has… raped you… hasn't he?'

She nodded her head.

Then, a tremor of hate towards his father invaded him, then he felt guilty.

'Oh! God! It's my fault! It's because I didn't go out of my room last night…'

'Do not think of this, but help me save myself!'

And Aliénor's ringed eyes begged him.

Then she cried with all her might:

'I do not want to see him ever again! I wish to return to the monastery, in order to hide my shame.'

'Oh, no!' Quentin replied. 'For he will dare look for you there. You need a safer hiding place.'

They began running through the forest, filled with dried leaves.

Quentin thought, then suddenly exclaimed:

'I know where to hide you, and you will be happy there. I will lead you to my uncle, my late mother's brother. My father will never dare attack the earl of Morenne.

My maternal grandfather had a fortress not far from here. He died three years ago, and his son, Jean inherited the fortress and the lands that came with it. Having fought next to emperor Frederick Barbarossa, he married a very nice lady, from the Outer-Rhine and they had five children. Unfortunately, they oldest son died prematurely of a bad fall from the horse, and they have suffered greatly. Even more so when they had three daughters afterwards. The two oldest girls have been married to neighboring lords. The third one, Rosemond, aged seventeen, is still with them. And seven years later, finally, a boy was born, Thibaut. It is he who is heir to the fortress and its lands.'

Poor Aliénor, exhausted, couldn't hear the history of the family that would take her in. She focused all her attention on not stumbling against the shrubs and rocks that lined the woods. Despite all, her tiredness took her and she let herself fall on a pile of leaves.

Quentin very tenderly lifted and carried her.

'Courage, my love, we will soon leave the woods and we will arrive on my uncle Jean's territory. You will feel safe.'

Aliénor didn't even react. In the arms of her loved one, she had the impression of finding herself on a moving cloud and she abandoned herself to this wellbeing, unknown to her. Her long black hair almost reached the ground.

Finally, they left the woods and took a right. There, the road became easier and Quentin let out a sigh of relief. This didn't escape the young girl who decide to walk on her own.

'My darling Quentin, I do not want to tire you. I think I got a little of my strength back.'

'Are you sure?'

'Yes.'

Then, she came to her feet and Quentin helped her advance by holding her arm.

After a mile, through the mists of the autumnal day, they saw the fortress of Morenne from afar, perched on a hill.

Quentin let out a cry of joy.

'We are finally there, my darling! Look there! It is my uncle's castle.'

When they arrived at the drawbridge, the guards recognised Quentin, for he had often come to his uncle's during his childhood and adolescence. He had shared lots of games with his cousin, who had left too early.

As soon as they entered his fortress, Jean of Morenne understood at once that something terrible must have happened. If not, Quentin would have let him know of his coming.

'I ask your forgiveness, uncle, for appearing here unannounced. I will give the reasons why later. Can you welcome us between your walls, my fiancée and I?'

'But of course, you are welcome!' Jean answered.

'I present you my fiancée, Aliénor of Scéry, who lived with us in my father's fortress.'

Aliénor could barely bow, she was so tired!

Irma, countess of Morenne, immediately noticed and hurried to invite her to sit down.

'Come, dear Aliénor, sit on this sofa,' she softly said.

The young girl collapsed on it.

'Maybe it would be better if she lay down?' She corrected. 'For she seems exhausted.

So she called for a servant.

'Fanchon! Lead this lady in an unoccuppied room.'

Barely extended, Aliénor fell into a deep sleep, or more precisely in a black hole, free of dreams.

After the young girl's departure, Quentin swallowed a liqueur to warm himself and to recuperate his forces. He sat down on an armchair of green velvet, that matched the tapestries that covered the walls of the main room where they were. And he told them:

'Now, uncle and aunt, I need to confess what brought us to you.'

The earl Jean, gave to understand Rosemond and Thibaut, his young children, that they had to leave the room. Under Irma's order, the nurse came to take them to the park.

Quentin began talking about the difficult return among his own, his opposition to his father who wished him to marry the marquis' daughter, in order to restore their coat of arms. He explained that he loved Aliénor and that the love was mutual. He told of his stupid battle with his father and recounted the horrible drama of which Aliénor had been victim.

'But all this is terrible!' Irma was outraged. 'What are you planning to do?'

'What I would wish, my dear aunt, would be for you to accept hosting Aliénor. She must remain hidden so my father doesn't marry her. And before my great distress, I thought of you, who have a generous heart.'

Then, the young man had to briefly explain the reasons Aliénor had been confided to his father, several years before.

'But of course,' she answered, 'for I can well put myself in her place. She hasn't been spoiled by fate.'

'You have done very well,' said the earl in his turn. 'But I think you would have done better to avoid battling your father. You know well you must respect him, even he shows himself to be obnoxious.'

'Unfortunately! Uncle, there are facts we can not forgive. Do you remember what your poor sister Mahaut had to suffer, due to my father's merciless harshness?'

'Yes,' Jean nodded, 'it is why he has never come here again, well knowing I would immediately send him away.'

Irma, whose sensibility was great, added:

'I think, unfortunately, that your father has committed this violation with the goal of making Aliénor his own. Maybe he thought that afterwards, she would accept to become his wife.'

'Well, he was strongly mistaken!'

All three remained in a moment of silence, immersed in their thoughts. Then the earl turned toward Quentin.

'You can stay here as well, if you so wish.'

'I sincerely thank you, uncle. I will maybe stay for a few days in your company, until Aliénor passes over the shock she has received. My presence will be necessary to her. Then, I have the intention of visiting my sister, whom I haven't seen since my return to Lanicey.'

'We understand perfectly. And rest assured, your fiancée will be treated like one of our daughters.'

At the end of a few days, Aliénor regained her strength. She had a little more appetite to eat Lucette, the cook's succulent meals: cabbage soup, bread kneaded every morning and baked in the great oven of the kitchen, venison of all sorts. In fact, the earl adored to hunt, his favorite pasttime. The young girl's cheeks colored again with vermilion, making her resemble a rose.

Quentin slowly took her out of the fortress, in the park, where a small chapel could be found. In this peaceful place, she prayed with all her heart, kneeling at the feet of the Virgin. When she got up, she felt comforted. Then they crossed the village where the poor peasants turned to admire her beauty. She finally took a love for life again.

Quentin decided to leave as soon as she felt well, and part of this family. After saying his goodbyes and hugging tightly dear Aliénor to him, he mounted his horse and left, without stopping at his father's.

When he arrived in Nevers, he was surprised by the view which reflected the economic development of the county. Everywhere he saw many groves separated by thickets well planted.

Still, it was a very hilly region, and his horse often labored to climb some of the very steep coast.

Arriving at the foot of the Vauze forterss, he sopped for a moment to contemplate it. Like the lord, he admired it, but found it less austere than that of Lanicey. Everywhere around, small villages dependent on it were found. He crossed a very beautiful park that embellished the castle. Quentin was in a hurry to meet this duke, a friend of the lord, that had managed to seduce his sister! Yet, the latter had a strong character.

As soon as she saw her brother that trotted in the park, Lidwine gave a cry a joy and ran to welcome him. She cried:

'Quentin! My dear Quentin! You are becoming more and more beautiful!'

He tied his horse and threw himself into her arms.

'And you, my dear sister, how you have transformed!'

Effectively, maternity rendered her radiant. She wore a bun held by a thin veil and her clothes, very elegant, masked well her state. She was proud of carrying a child that would be the joy of their couple.

Lidwine made him enter by holding his hand and led him into the living room where the duke was.

'Come, I will present you to Othon, my dear husband who makes me so happy!'

Othon rose and said:

'You are welcome here, dear baron.'

Quentin made him his best bow, but the duke stopped him.

'We are part of the same family now, let us not formalise ourselves.'

'I agree with you, then call me by my name.'

'Understood.'

Quentin thought that his brother in law had a beautiful presence, while still remaining natural. And he thought that, for once, his father had made a beautiful act in organizing this union.

Lidwine showed him the castle. Othon had made numerous reparations, thanks to his wife's dowry: the roof had been reinforced, the stables had become bigger, the dovecote, collapsed in the yard of the fortified house, had been rebuilt.

The prison that Godefroy had visited and admired still existed, but Lidwine had obtained the pardon of the prisoners. This place served as a cellar now, filled with delicious wine barrels.

At the interior of the room reigned a very nice atmosphere, thanks to the good taste of the young woman. She had put orange and yellow hangings on the walls of each piece, which gave them a bright light, even in the absence of the sun. Pretty trinkets adorned the chests and trunks brought by the duke mainly from the Middle East. Everywhere, autumn bouquets of flowers brightened the tables. Magnificent chandeliers were put on massive wood furniture. Lidwine, all happy, showed him a small wicker basket for the baby, to lie within.

'I am certain this baby will be a boy', said Othon, satisfied to finally have an heir.

'I truly wish it for you', answered Quentin, smiling.

The duke waved a big bell, to call a servant.

'Jeanette, bring us a cake of your making, accompanied by an excellent wine.'

'Very well, duke.'

The servant quickly brought them a cake with apples, cooked to perfection and poured them a drink.

Then Lidwine, always curious to know all, addressed her brother:

'Tell us, dear Quentin, have you found a fiancée at Dijon?'

The young man noticed that his sister hadn't changed: matters of the heart especially interested her.

'No', he somberly answered.

She began to laugh at once.

He hesitated before admitting:

'No, for it is elsewhere that I have the chosen of my heart.'

'Then, quickly tell me. Do I know her?'

'You know her for sure: it is your friend Aliénor of Scéry.'

Lidwine clapped her hands, then ran to embrace him.

'Oh! I am so happy!' She said. 'You couldn't have chosen better. Does she love you as well?'

'Yes, of course.'

'And what does our father say?'

Quentin remained silent for a moment, not knowing how to tell them the terrible news.

'Alas!' He answered sighing, 'our father wants to marry her as well.'

Lidwine jumped from the chair and cried:

'What? But he is completely mad!'

The young man knew well his sister would understand. So he told her all that had happened, his rebellion against his father, then the rape of his dear Aliénor, whom he had hidden at his uncle's, the earl of Morenne.

'Our father is a criminal!' Cried Lidwine.

At that moment, the duke, who had listened to their conversation without saying anything, thought it best to intervene.

'Excuse me for interrupting, but I do not consider rape a crime.'

Lidwine threw him a furious look.

'Ah! I see you think like a man, to whom all is allowed and know that you disappoint me greatly.'

That was the first quarrel the young spouses had. And Quentin became sad.

The duke followed:

'I easily admit this act is detestable, but the lord remains a friend to me. You must know this as well.'

Othon wanted to get up to leave the room, but Lidwine held him back.

'Come, dear, let us not be upset. It would, in my opinion, be more important to look for a solution to help Aliénor come out of her painful situation.'

'I would gladly help her, but I do not know how.'

The duke drank another glass of wine. Sometimes, alcohol stimulated him. But he never abused.

They each thought in silence, then Othon said:

'I can try to visit my friend, and try to make him abandon this marriage idea.'

'Oh, yes!' Exclaimed Quentin, 'it is an excellent idea, for you are his friend, and maybe he'll listen to you.'

Sixth part

The duke of Sacht sent a messenger to Lanicey to inform Godefroy of his visit in about a week. But he did not say why.

Godefroy was very intrigued, for his son in law and friend wouldn't just come to visit him now that he was fulfilled by his marriage and the near arrival of an heir. Still, he was always happy to receive him, remembering he owed him his life.

Quentin hadn't come back to the fortress since their altercation, but Godefroy doubted his son hid himself somewhere in company of Aliénor, and this rendered him furious. Yes, he had not accepted Aliénor's departure since the day she had become his by force. His male ego had been flouted once again. And still, he thought that if Aliénor came back to him, he would be very happy, for he had really fallen in love with her. He remembered her splendid body of voluptuous shapes, her velvety cheeks like the petals of a rose, her superb black and brilliant hair. He felt tormented by desire, like a young man. Just like his son, he remained haunted by Aliénor's image, whose nude body had shined under the storm's lightning.

When the duke entered the reception hall of the fortress, preceded by an obsequious servant, Godefroy opened his arms, like in the past. He made him sit in his best armchair, covered in a very thick velvet.

He ordered a servant to bring them a good wine, then he sat down in front of his friend.

'Then, dear friend!' He said. 'It is very nice of you to visit me, for after the leaving of my children, I feel alone here.'

Othon appeared surprised.

'Then your son has left as well?'

'Yes. To you, whom I consider a friend, I can well confide. Quentin left me after a violent discussion between us.'

'What about?'

'Oh! This will make you laugh, image that I have the intention of remarrying, so I will know better days in my old age. Loneliness weighs me presently. Or, Quentin opposed this completely.'

'And for what reason?'

'He thinks I am too old and I am not capable of making a woman happy anymore. However, I still feel very young!' He added with a guttural laugh.

Othon did not want to contradict him. He asked:

'Why? Have you met a rich countess that has recently become widowed?'

'No, the deuce! I would rather have a fresh and innocent lady, even penniless. Her charms will be enough.'

The duke tapped him friendly on the shoulder, but followed:

'Come, dear Godefroy, I thought you did not trust the ladies anymore! Do you not fear of being betrayed by this young person that all men would admire?'

'It is true', admitted the lord, 'that I was very jealous in the past. But I have changed with time. Furthermore, the one I will marry will be above all suspicion.'

'Does this mean you know her well?' Asked Othon, feigning surprise.

Here, the sire reared.

'Confound it! I found you very curious! If this is the goal of your visit, I will say nothing. Do you think, like my son, I am incapable of love? If so, hurry and join him! Without doubt you know where he is?'

'No, absolutely not.'

Godefroy got up abruptly, taken by a sudden impatience. He hated being judged, especially by a special friend. His face became red, his eyes narrowed and his hands trembled with indignation.

So he resorted to a trick: he struck the ground with the heel of his boot three times, which made Ulric appear, who was in the room underneath.

This one came as soon as he could, after making a low bow and said:

'My lord and master, I must inform you that the guards have seen unknown men galloping in the distance in our direction. Maybe they are bandits or invaders? What must we do?'

Godefroy answered with an authoritative voice:

'I thank you for letting me know. You are truly a good servant! I will go up to the tower myself and give orders.'

Ulric smoothly retired, with a mischievous smile.

'My dear Othon,' said the sire, 'you see me in the obligation of leaving you.'

'But I understand perfectly. Duty calls.'

'It is a pity, for I appreciated your visit. I wish you a good return, and most of all, do not forget to kiss my dear Lidwine.'

Quentin went back to his uncle, after having stayed a night at the duke of Sacht's. He had to rest, as well as his horse. He had seen how happy Lidwine was, and he found it unjust that he was not. Just like Aliénor felt, he was horrified by his father and he galloped before the Lanicey fortress without stopping.

At the Morenne castle, he was warmly welcomed by his family. Aliénor hung around his neck like a branch, and he felt her huge need to be loved and protected. His heart melted before her and he had to control his body, he wanted her so much! But he knew he had to wait for their marriage before having her. He did not want to behave like his father.

A month passed, in the course of which Quentin gave his uncle a helping hand with the management of his properties. In fact, he replaced, while ignoring it, his deceased cousin.

Irma was happy to notice that her protégée, Aliénor blossomed gradually. They found themselves often in the living room and talked about everything and nothing. The countess gave her the gift of many dresses she could no longer wear, having taken on some weight. Aliénor wore them wonderfully, being slim, and this enhanced her beauty.

Rosemonde, aged seventeen, admired her greatly, and soon made her her confidante.

While walking together in the castle's park, Rosemonde often led her new friend to the stables.

'Do you ride?' She asked Aliénor one day.

'No, I have never learned.'

'Do you wish to learn? I know someone who would be happy to teach you.'

Aliénor did not hide her surprise.

'Oh, really? Who is it?'

Rosemonde suddenly seemed to hesitate:

'If I tell you, could you keep it a secret?'

'Of course! Aren't we like sisters?'

The girl almost whispered.

'Look: it's about the groom. He is Lucette's son, who managed to make him work for us. I have never seen a more beautiful man than him! And…'

It was Aliénor who finished.

'And you have fallen in love.'

'How do you know? It's true, I can't stop thinking about him. Then, I often come to pick flowers, for I must pass the stable to get to the garden. And in summer, I come every day looking for my horse to go for a stroll, in company of my cousin. He smiles to me very time.'

'Rosemonde, you are a hussy! I suppose your parents know nothing,'

Rosemone sighed.

'No, but sometimes, I am dying to reveal it. For they plan to make me marry this cousin I have always known, whom I will never love. While you, Aliénor, you know how it is to love and be loved by a man you like.'

'Yes', She admitted. 'It is a chance, really.'

Then she hurried to change the subject.

'It's a little chilly, don't you think so? Winter is approaching and I think it will snow. Let's go back to get warm.'

Othon wrote a long letter to Quentin to tell him about the visit to the lord, visit that had been a failure, since his friend continued in his wish to remarry. He said the lord had no idea where Quentin was hiding and that Aliénor could still feel safe at the earl of Morenne.

December was approaching and since about a fortnight, Aliénor felt tired. She got up later, slept a lot and showed signs of inexplicable melancholy. She painfully swallowed the always hearty meals of which Lucette had the secret. Her cheeks paled and dark circles were outlined under her huge eyes, that she held downcast. Quentin noticed and softly asked is she was suffering. But Aliénor shook her head. As the days passed, she became more closed, like a flower at dawn. She refused to walk in company of Rosemonde, giving as excuse the cold outside. Previously, the girl did not show sings of suffering from the cold.

Every evening, the castle's inhabitants gathered in front of the fireplace where a fire crackled merrily and each, in turn, told a story. Most of the stories were from very old legends, transmitted orally from generation to generation. And as time passed, they slowly transformed. Everyone appreciated this time of relaxation and dreaming at the end of the day. Quentin and Rosemonde excelled in this, that required good memory and imagination.

But when Aliénor's turn came, not only did she refuse to participate, she went to her chamber crying. Quentin was very worried, thinking of a grave illness that had taken his fiancée, like a curse from Heaven.

Irma as well, was dismayed, for she thought of Aliénor like her own daughter.

One day when they were alone in the living room, the countess asked her gently:

'What happened, my dear one? I see you are suffering. Can you not confide in me? I will keep your secret, believe me.'

The young girl lowered her head and remained silent.

'Do you think Quentin is ignoring you while helping my husband?'

She shook her head no, then answered softly as not to wound her.

'No. Do not insist further, please.'

Then she took refuge in her room.

One day, Irma received the visit of her oldest daughter, Guenièvre, mother of two adorable children.

Guenièvre knew Aliénor's past and had already had the chance to sympathize with her in the past months.

The countess expressed her worry concerning Aliénor, who had changed so much!

And Guenièvre, very pragmatic, said:

'This young girl wouldn't be pregnant, since unfortunately, she has been raped?'

Good Irma gasped.

'Oh! Heavens! I hope not!'

Her face became pale due to shock.

'And if this is true, how can we be sure? We can not have her examined by a midwife, for she will be very shocked.'

A little while after this conversation, the servant committed to Aliénor's care, noticed she had more and more trouble clothing her mistress. Her shirts were becoming too narrow at the chest, as well as the hips. And naively, the little maid said:

'Without offending you, madam, don't you find you have become bigger? Couldn't you be pregnant?'

Aliénor gave her a look of profound distress and exclaimed, horrified:

'But no! This can not be, I have simply put on weight.'
Ninette said nothing, and kept her opinion to herself.

The next morning, Aliénor sent Ninette away, saying she was feeling better and could clothe herself.

The young woman knew she had become pregnant, but she denied this harsh reality that brought her back to the evening when the lord had raped her. Every night, she cried in silence, in her bed. She had to hide this shameful state. But until when could she do it? For this pregnancy would become visible before its term was over. And what would she do with this child that she absolutely rejected?

She dreamed one time that the lord had found her at Morenne and he had forced her to marry him, for he knew she was carrying his child. She woke up screaming in fright...

Then one day she stopped crying, for a soothing idea had come to her: she had remembered a small servant working at the Lanicey fortress, who had become pregnant at thirteen, who had gotten rid of the baby after giving birth. She had learned this young girl had dropped her baby in a facility of abandon, at Dijon. Curious, Aliénor had inquired about this to a maid. This one had explained that the tower was meant to gather abandoned children. When a mother didn't want to keep her baby, she could take it to a church equipped with an abandoning tower: this tower consisted of a cylinder opening at the exterior of the church, like the drum of a door. The mother placed the child in the cylinder and turned it so the child would go to the interior of the church. Then she rang a bell that that could be heard in the church and someone came to take the child. Then, the baby would be placed in an orphanage.

During her night of insomnia, Aliénor thought that this solution was the only one for her, with Quentin's support. But she did not dare reveal yet her state to her fiancé, knowing him anxious.

Then, one day came when, very weak, she stumbled and missed two steps while going down the stairs. She unfortunately fell on her belly and felt a violent pain before fainting. She had to stay in bed a long time, as she became highly feverish. Ninette made her swallow potions made of plants, and watched over her day and night. Quentin was very frightened of losing her. Finally, her fever went down and at the end of one month, the young girl could get up. Without wanting it, she had gotten rid of this shameful pregnancy which had so mortified her!

When Aliénor healed, she seemed to come alive, to Irma's and Quentin's great joy, who had been so worried about her life. She went out to get some air, even if in February, the days were still cold and her cheeks colored again. She went to the small chapel of the fortress, and thanked the Virgin fervently to have delivered her from this evil that had so made her suffer!

Wanting to express her gratitude to Irma, she proposed to go to market that was held in the village next to theirs. She had the impression of being a little part of the daily lives of her hosts. The market, taking place every Monday, Irma accepted, thinking that it will do Aliénor a lot of good.

Some days after Christmas, a messenger crossed the drawbridge of the Morenne fortress to bring a message to the earl. He had come from very far, from Nevers. The earl hurriedly unrolled the fold and after having read it, uttered a cry of joy. Everyone gathered around him to know the content of the letter.

This message was from the duke of Sacht and Lidwine, who were informing them of the birth of their son, Conrad, born on December 30, 1196 in Var.

« Everything went well, even though Lidwine regretted her mother's absence to assist with this birth. Conrad and his mother are well. We have found an excellent nurse. We are delighted.

92

We kiss you all, without forgetting Quentina and Aliénor.

Othon and Lidwine »

The letter went from hand to hand, and everyone was raptured.

'I am so happy for Lidwine, so honest and full of life!' Said Irma.

'Yes, she deserves to be happy', added the earl.

Then, he turned to Quentin.

'Your father is now a grandfather and I hope he will abandon the idea of remarrying.'

'I am not certain', replied the young baron. 'I know my father well and I know he often materializes his plans.'

'Then let him marry Bertille of Attrans himself!' cried Aliénor.

'You are right indeed, my dear', approved Quentin. And he passionately kissed his fiancée.

As it was very cold and the messenger was covered in snow, Irma proposed softly to host him during the night, which the servant did not refuse. So he went to join earl Morenne's servants, at the last floor of the fortress. And there, he found a friend, Wilfried, who had once served at the baron of Lanicey's, named 'Godefroy, the cruel'. They talked for a long time, remembering, before going to bed.

Wilfried had married Fanchon, a servant of the earl of Morenne and had left his post to follow her to the earl's.

Or, Wilfried knew Ulric, both having grown up in the same village. Once Othon's messenger had rested and left for Var, Wildfried felt the need to know news about his old master, lord Lanicey. Ulric wasn't difficult to find, given that he spent his moments of rest in a seedy gambling den, situated between the two fortresses, named 'In the right spout'. This pub was mainly frequented by peasants and tradespeople.

When he wanted to meet him, Wilfried asked the earl's permission to go out to meet his son who was coming back from Besançon. But in truth, he went to 'In the right spout', where wine freely flowed. Even if the interior of the pub was quite sombre, for the light was scarce in winter, he recognised Ulric who hid his baldness under a hat, who seemed tired and was bellowing a song to drink. He was sitting with a waitress with which he appeared to be flirting, because she seemed delighted. When he spotted Wilfried, he got up to his to his table and told him:

'Hello, old brother! What are you doing here?' Then he added.

'But since you are here, I will offer you a glass!'

'I will accept, thank you. I come to see you so you will give me news of the Lanicey fortress.'

'Oh, oh!' Cried the bandit. Are you regretting the time when we were making good things together?'

'Not at all,' Wilfried answered, 'because with Fanchon I had to settle down. No, I would like for you to tell me how your master is, the old baron. Is he still as merciless with the house people? We had named him 'Godefroy, the cruel.'

Ulric began laughing like a rattle.

'He hasn't changed! Me, I have nothing to complain about, for I have it well. But others, especially old Hilda, they have it tough! Especially since his son has left him.'

And Wilfried, ignoring the secret, answered:

'Still, he is not far: he lives with us, with his future wife.'

Ulric leaped with joy, for he finally knew where Aliénor was hiding! He sent his hat in the air, discovering his smooth skull, and his whole face transformed in a cluster of wrinkles, he was laughing so hard!

'Ah! You are a true friend to me.'

'Why?' Asked the other, surprised.

'Nothing. Because I am happy to see you again.'

And he whistled to the waitress.

'Darling, bring us something more to drink.'

When she came, clothed in a large dress, Ulric pinched her backside.

'Serve us the best wine in this gambling den, the price does not matter!'

At the end of an hour, Wilfried, having drank so much he had trouble getting up, left for home.

Back at the Lanicey fortress, Ulric hastened to fetch his master. He joyously tapped at the door of his study, situated in the high tower.

'Enter!' Said a malicious and rough voice.

Inhabited by hatred, the sire had become disfigured: he didn't cut his beard, which had become white, and his grey eyes didn't shine brightly anymore. His mouth had collapsed more.

Ulric entered, his face radiant, and the lord doubted that his henchman had something of importance to tell him.

'Sit down and tell me everything', he cried in a voice which had become courteous.

'Oh! Master, I know where you ungrateful son is hiding.'

The lord jumped in his chair.

'Where is that scoundrel? It is high time I took my vengeance.'

'There is no need to go far!' Sneered the soulless man. 'He is hosted by Jean of Morenne, your former brother in law, in company of Aliénor.'

'Indeed, he is afraid of nothing, being welcomed by my most fierce enemy. But thanks to you, the hour of my vengeance approaches and it will be without pity. How did you find him?'

Ulric told him about his meeting with Wilfried at 'In the right spout'.

'This is good work!' Exclaimed Godegroy, all joyous.

'What do you plan to do now?'

'I must think.

'If you need me, do not hesitate', said the terrible superintendent. 'You know I can second you in all your endeavours.'

'Yes, I will call for you for sure.'

Godefroy had also received the duke of Sacht's messenger, and the announcement of the birth of his nephew flattered his ego. So, his illustrious line continued.

In the month that followed, the weather softened a little. The snow had melted, which was extremely rare for this time of the year. So he decided to go to Var to admire little Conrad. He cut his beard and smoothed his tousled hair. He left at dawn and had himself driven in a sleigh, for the roads remained bad.

He arrived just before nightfall. Lidwine welcomed him with benevolence, but didn't show any real joy. For her, he remained her mother's assassin.

In exchange, the duke showed himself happy by this unexpected visit, Godefroy being his friend.

Conrad was taken out of a little basket and shown before the lord at the light of a candle. Then he began crying with such a vigour that Godefroy exclaimed:

'Ah! He is well. He already has character, this little one. We will make a brave knight out of him, just like his father.'

'And like his grandfather', added Othon laughing. 'I think he resembles his mother a lot, for he is very beautiful.'

'Yes!' said Godefroy, who had the feeling of seeing Quentin after his birth.

Suddenly, the door to the room opened and a charming young woman that the lord did not know came in. So he bowed before her, out of politeness.

'Dear friend', said Othon, 'I present you a cousin, madam Isadora of Willeim, who came to visit us, like you.'

'I am most very pleased', said the lord.

'So am I', she graciously replied.

Godefroy examined her closely, undressed her with a look, then thought her pretty.

Obviously, she didn't have Aliénor's sublime beauty, of which he thought with rage, for she had dared escape him. But she was agreeable to look at. Isadora wore two long blond braids, framing a face with fine lines. Big, elegantly clothed with a black dress that highlighted the whiteness of her skin, he liked her anyway.

'Where do you come from, madam?'

'From afar. I live in the Alsace county.'

'It is why we are hosting her now', Lidwine explained. 'And we get along very well, don't we Isa?'

'It's true. Your son is adorable!'

They went to the table and the lord devoured a succulent meal composed of cabbage and poultry. An excellent wine was also served. The fireplace emanated a delicious warmth that made Godefroy sleepy. The duke proposed him to pass the night with them, which he gladly accepted.

The next morning, the lord woke up early to leave for Lanicey. But Othon asked him to stay for breakfast.

He took the chance to question his friend about Isadora, to find out if he liked her.

'I do not know her enough', answered Godefroy, with a detached tone.

Then the duke told him she had become a widow three years ago and she had a son of then years of age.

'How old is she?' He asked of curiosity.

'She is thirty, but she seems younger. Her husband left her a good inheritance, for he was a marquis.'

'Well, good for her!'

The duke hesitated an instant before saying.

'Maybe you could marry her? You have given me Lidwine, then in my turn, I can give you my cousin.'

But the baron made as if he hadn't heard.

After drinking a bowl of warm milk, he prepared to leave. He said his goodbyes to the family and called for his driver to take him back home.

In his study, Godefroy thought at length of his vengeance directed against Aliénor. Just like Mahaut, she had flouted him with his own son! When he only thought of making her happy by marrying her. He was brooding with bitterness, knowing she lived surrounded and received by the Morenne family.

Equally, he felt a mad rage against Quentin who had proven stronger than him. And he thought that only Aliénor's disappearance could punish his son and avenge him at the same time.

When he had thought good and well at his decision, at the end of a month, he decided to call for Ulric. He grabbed his big bell and furiously waved it.

'You called, master?'

'Yes, I still need you to make a dirty work.'

Ulric, seated in front of him, patiently waited for his orders.

'Look: like you know, I am furious against Aliénor who refused to marry me because she preferred Quentin. And she must be punished in a radical way. I wish, just like in Mahaut's case, to show myself merciless! Do you understand what I await from you?'

Godefroy got up and paced the room, sign of a great feverishness.

The man without heart had clearly understood, but not one of his face muscles moved. He was impassable, as usual. By dint of frequenting loose women, his face was covered in pimples.

He simply asked:

'By what means should I realise your will?'

'I think that, firstly, you will hide yourself in the vicinity of their fortress, without making yourself known by the guards. I know you are cunning enough for that. Then you will try to find out the comings and goings of Aliénor. If she goes to the village, for example, mark the days when she goes out alone. We do not need any witnesses.'

'Assuming', said the thug. 'And then, what should I do?'

The lord raised his arm and made a circular gesture.

'You will do what the devil will command you!'

And saying these words, he slammed his fist on the table. By this gesture, Godefroy felt the feeling of decapitating his thought and felt relieved.

'Of course', he recalled him, 'you will act in the utmost secrecy. Swear it to me!'

'I swear, master! Do not worry.'

Ulric hid himself in the small forest that surrounded the Morenne fortress. He stayed there for several days and could observe the life of the inhabitants of the castle. He saw Quentin leave for a hunt with his uncle. He equally saw Aliénor, but a young girl accompanied her during her walks. Still, with the exception of Monday mornings, when she went alone to the neighboring village.

Then, a machiavellian smile flashed on his ugly face. Next Monday was a wonderful spring day. The trees were beginning to flower and all of nature was in agitation.

When Aliénor entered the small forest to go to the market, the man without heart followed slyly, while hiding behind fir trees.

The young girl entered the little forest with her ondulating gait. She finally felt happy, for the earl of Morenne had told her about her marriage with Quentin. All the servants were boiling, for this marriage would be celebrated in a month.

«By God! She is a fine piece!» thought Ulric.

But he had to accomplish his dirty work. When she was far away enough from the fortress, he advanced slowly *behind her, held his breath, stretched his bow and fired. Then he hid behind the trunk of a big oak.*

Aliénor uttered a loud cry of pain that no one heard, except himself and the birds huddled in their nests. Quickly, before her eyes, the sky began to obscure, then became black, then she had the impression of floating in the clouds. Finally, she swayed and slid to the earth, bathed in a pool of blood.

The man without heart left without even looking at her.

At the Morenne castle, the cook waited for Aliénor's return, to begin preparing the meal. She was surprised by the lateness of her return. Then, after an hour, Lucette went to warn the countess.

Irma questioned the guards to know if she had come back. They assured her they had seen the young girl go out toward the forest, but she hadn't come back…

Alarmed, the countess went to warn Quentin who was trying to revive the fire in the fireplace. When he learned his loved one hadn't returned, he was so distraught that he felt a pain in his heart. Having a bad feeling, he ran to the forest calling Aliénor with all his might. Only the crunches of the branches answered him.

Suddenly, he saw a young girl lying on the earth, an arrow planted in her back. She had lost a lot of blood and her magnificent eyes had become dull. Her long black hair was scattered around her, like the petals of a flower...

He cried with pain and remained next to her for a long time.

Jean de Morenne finally came and raised Quentin saying: 'She is with God, she suffers no more. Come, my child!'

Ulric came before his master and said he had accomplished his will. Godfrey heard the fact without flinching.

'Are you certain no one saw you?' He still asked.

'Absolutely certain, sire.'

Thinking, he saw her goddess like body that he had coveted and that he had had only once, by force.

100

His face hardened, he proudly straightened his head and, in an unwavering voice, replied:

'This is very well! I thank you.'

Then he went back to work.

Two months later, he received a letter from the duke of Sacht, telling him this:

« *My dear Godefroy,*

It is with immense pain we must tell you about the death of Aliénor, your protégée, which came last March, while she was residing with the earl of Morenne. One day when she was going to the neighboring village, a stranger willingly killed her with an arrow, leaving Quentin sorely tested.

To survive this pain, your son has enrolled in the army of our emperor of the Saint Empire, Henri VI. No one knows if he'll come back.

We will keep you informed.

Do not hesitate to come back to see us. You will be welcomed with all the courtesy you are due.

Your devoted son-in-law and friend,

Othon de Sacht. »

After thinking for a moment, Godefroy decided to respond favorably to this charming invitation, for the idea came to him to negotiate his remarriage with Isadora of Willeim.